Songs of the Seven

GELFLING CLANS

J. M. LEE

PENGUIN YOUNG READERS LICENSES
An Imprint of Penguin Random House LLC, New York

Illustrations by Brian Froud, Pippa Broadhurst, Ryan DaSilva,
Tim Napper, Jon McCoy, Max Berman, and Cyrille Nomberg.

Photo credits: used throughout: (background paper 1) donatas1205/Shutterstock.com,
(background paper 2), Lukasz Szwaj/Shutterstock.com, (background paper 3) Paladin12/Shutterstock.
com, (ink bleed) AnjeseAnna/Shutterstock.com, (picture frame) Miloje/Shutterstock.com, (torn paper)
vesna cvorovic/Shutterstock.com; vi, 28, 61, 90, 119, 153, 183: (ripped paper tag) ESB Professional/
Shutterstock.com; 1, 29, 62, 91, 120, 154, 184: (leather tag) donatas1205/Shutterstock.com; 126–7, 150–1:
(wind pattern) Wenpei/Shutterstock.com; 128–9: (air and fire pattern) charodijko/Shutterstock.com;
132–3: (wave pattern) Benjavisa Ruangvaree Art/Shutterstock.com; 146–7, 164–5: (space vector art)
Melok/Shutterstock.com; 194–5: (abstract wave lines) korkeng/Shutterstock.com; 196–7:
(summer landscape) makar/Shutterstock.com; 196–9: (blue watercolor background)
ESB Professional/Shutterstock.com

Published in 2020 by Penguin Young Readers Licenses, an imprint of
Penguin Random House LLC, New York. Manufactured in China.

Visit us online at www.penguinrandomhouse.com.

ISBN 9780593095591   10 9 8 7 6 5 4 3 2 1

Songs of the Seven

GELFLING CLANS

J. M. LEE

Introduction

In my youth, I dreamed of walking the many paths of Thra, from the shadowy trails intertwined among the trees of the Endless Forest to the snowy cliffs that give way to the Silver Sea. And yet, on the eve of my fated departure, traveling pack on my shoulders and Firca at my breast, I found myself afraid. Afraid of the unknown that lay beyond the green leaves I had always called home, but more than that, afraid that once I had left, I might never find my way back.

But I could not bow to the fear and hold it in my heart forever. By the light of the Rose Sun, I left the place where my mother and her mother and her mother had lived happily and died peacefully, and set out to pursue my destiny: to witness as much of the world as I could, and to fill my ears and heart with as many songs as others might deign to tell. To dream-etch every scent and sight; to commit every wonder to memory.

My naive quest was to seek out the Gelfling—scattered across the land in seven clans, each more reclusive than the last. The Stonewood, deep in the Endless Forest. The Spriton, in the open plains. The Drenchen, in the far southern swamps. The Vapra, in the blustery cold north. The Dousan, wandering in the Crystal Desert. The Sifa, sailing upon the Silver Sea. And the Grottan, hiding deep within the mountains.

It took most of my life, and I do not regret a single day. With the Brother Suns and the Sister Moons as my guides, I sought out the seven clans. I met with their younglings and their elders. I sat with their maudras. I listened to their songs. I saw my life divided into seven chapters, each lived with one of our mighty clans so that I might finally uncover the whole that is made up of our seven parts.

That was many trine ago. Now, I look upon my records as if they were adventures had by someone else. And they were; the youth who charged, fresh-faced, into unknown lands was a Gelfling wholly different from the one who writes this introduction, looking back. My heart is full of songs and memories, my fingers burning with the makings of one final dream-etching. And brightest is a spot in my forehead, not unlike Mother Aughra's third eye. It yearns to open and spill out all I have seen, all I have learned, so that the experience might not be trapped within only one mind forever.

And so, I arrange this collection for you. All I have learned and loved of our proud and gentle ways: this teller's songs of the seven clans.

Thriya

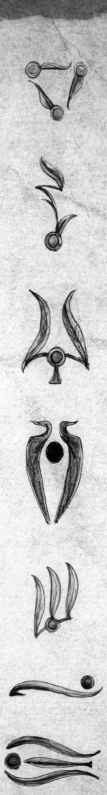

THE STONEWOOD CLAN

Stonewood Village

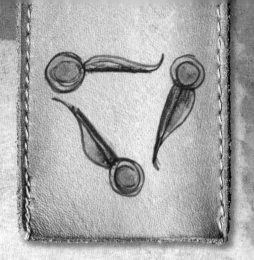

Within the dark Endless Forest that fills the
Skarith Basin like moss in a cupped hand, there
is a mound of stones piled as high as the trees.
Moss and vines and roots weave the boulders
together, making them one. Making them whole.
And there it stands, at the foot of a clear lake,
for all to see: Bolentor, the Stone Tower. Or, as it
has come to be known by Gelfling far and wide,
Stone-in-the-Wood.

Spilling out from the rocky rise is the village that the Stonewood clan calls
home. Nestled in the wealth of the abundant forest and with the lake at its
back, Stone-in-the-Wood is everything a woodland-dwelling Gelfling might
dream of. This is the place where I was born—the place where my journey
began.

We Stonewood Gelfling are known for our toughness and bravery, traits that
are required to live in the eat-or-be-eaten world of the Endless Forest, where
no Gelfling sits at the top of the food chain. The Stonewood take pride in
their reputation, and as a community, they enjoy encouraging one another,
even during competitive sports. While I believe that reducing a clan to a
few attributes is foolhardy—no one is ever one thing or another just because
of their clan affiliation—I can safely say we Stonewood go out of our way
to emphasize our hardiness and courage, especially when interacting with
Gelfling from other clans.

Like all Gelfling clans, the Stonewood have a clan-first mentality. When I was young and faced with decisions for the future, I would turn to my clan for guidance. No matter whom I asked, the answer always began with "What's best for the clan?" Although this way of thinking taught me to prioritize the Stonewood and set aside the well-being of other Gelfling clans, I found, after my later travels, that this clan-centric philosophy may—ironically—be one of the few concepts that the seven clans have in common.

DAILY LIFE

Stone-in-the-Wood is a large, industrious community, with daily roles carefully assigned by our maudra and her elder council in order to maintain a prosperous, thriving clan. Among the Stonewood are blacksmiths, woodcrafters, stoneworkers, fire keepers, gardeners, hunters, and a dozen other specialists who all work together, day after day. The work within the community is balanced, oral tradition and wisdom are passed down, and the clan remains strong, healthy, and happy.

Many are surprised to find that my parents were not song tellers but wayfinders. Their role among the Stonewood was to aid travelers in their journey, sometimes leaving for days at a time to guide others through the Endless Forest. As a youngling, I accompanied them many times on their journeys. These adventures with my family inspired some of my favorite songs.

Days in Stone-in-the-Wood begin early in the morning—the first clang of the blacksmith's hammer signifies the start to a new day. Those whose work takes them outside the bounds of the village say their goodbyes and depart; those whose work occupies them within the village meet in their groups to discuss the day's plan. Work continues until sunset, when the hearth is lit for a communal supper and, of course, a song or two. At night, the lanterns full of Firebugs are strung along the shell-roofed homes at the base of the rise. The flickering light of the lanterns makes it seem as though the village itself rests among the sparkling stars.

THE STONEWOOD
AND THE SKEKSIS LORDS

On the edge of the Endless Forest, the earth splits, and out sprouts a magnificent castle of black stone, like a claw reaching for the very suns: the Castle of the Crystal. Within its mighty halls dwell the Skeksis Lords, and may they do so forever that we might warm our faces in their radiant light. Indeed, it is thanks to them that such a fantastic structure even exists. From any place where a Gelfling might crane their head above the trees of the wood, they will see the tower of the castle, proof of the impossible power wielded by the Skeksis, and evidence of their ability to protect that which lies hidden within the castle's shining and hallowed walls.

While the Stonewood benefit from the natural bounty of the wood and the Black River, we also prosper from our proximity to the Skeksis. Many Stonewood are called to serve the Skeksis within the castle itself. This is an honor bestowed more frequently to Stonewood Gelfling than to Gelfling of any other clan. In my youth and into my young adulthood, I saw many younglings receive their invitation (though I never received one myself—song tellers are rarely called to serve as guards at the castle). I remember seeing my friends' faces brighten when they heard they had been called by name to walk among the Skeksis. It is an unparalleled task among Gelfling, and especially among the Stonewood, whose relationship with the Skeksis might be called more intimate than that of any other clan (aside from the Vapra).

This discrepancy does not go unnoticed by my clan. It is no secret that many Stonewood believe the Skeksis were in error when they chose the Vapra to be the leaders of the Gelfling and our ambassadors to the Skeksis. This is an idea I first heard before I could even hold my first flute, and one embedded in many Stonewood conversations, from passionate Gelfling venting their feelings over a cup of brew to my maudra herself when entertaining Vapran representatives from Ha'rar. Why was the Vapran Citadel chosen as the capital of the Gelfling when Stone-in-the-Wood is often called the hearth of the Skarith Land? The Stonewood maudra interacts with the Skeksis on a more frequent basis, and it is Stonewood Gelfling who are most commonly called to serve at the castle. So why was the Vapran maudra named All-Maudra? As a young Stonewood, it was natural to wonder why the Skeksis chose to favor the Vapra over our clan.

But it was even more important to know the dangers of disagreeing with the Skeksis. Not only because the Skeksis are much wiser and more powerful than us Gelfling, but also because mistrusting the Skeksis, and in turn the Vapra, might result in rivalries that could damage our livelihood and reputation. If the Vapra decided to challenge the Stonewood, it could mean fewer imports from the north, including any and all trade from the Sifa, who use Ha'rar as their primary trading port. Not to mention jeopardizing our long-earned rapport with the Skeksis . . . Whether or not the Skeksis were wrong in choosing the Vapra, accepting the circumstances as they are now may be the safest way to preserve the Stonewood clan's strong standing.

NAME DAY

While every Gelfling celebrates their Name Day in a different way, our
Stonewood Name Day tradition is very dear to me. While naming a Gelfling
and presenting the youngling is essentially the same as it is in other Gelfling
communities, the celebration of the first Name Day in Stone-in-the-Wood has
an additional ritual of passage.

When a youngling celebrates the sixth anniversary of their Name Day, they,
along with any other younglings whose Name Days fall within the same season,
are sent to climb Bolentor without the guidance of adults. Each youngling is
sent to the summit with a small chisel. When they reach the top, they find a
stone that fits their liking and carve a sigil into it. This becomes the sign of their
name, memorialized with the hundreds of other sigils carved before them.

I have such fond memories of my Name Day climb; I remember precisely the
spot where my sigil was carved. After so many trine, it is overgrown with moss
and vines. Yet during my many travels, knowing that my sign was still carved
atop Bolentor made me feel as though, no matter where I wandered, my home
always waited for me, there in Stone-in-the-Wood.

Stone and Wood

The Endless Forest is dense, and it is the great equalizer of the Skarith Land; in order to live happily among the other creatures of the wood that are strong of tooth and nail, we Stonewood have, quite appropriately, honed our stone- and wood-crafting skills into an art. These important trades are very similar, in that they take time to learn and even more time to execute. Training trees and other wood life to grow in specific shapes can occupy the entirety of one woodcrafter's lifetime; doing the same with stone can take generations.

However difficult to master, these talents fortify the entire village from the ground up, perhaps most evident in the way they weave the stone, trees, and wood together to create a myriad of homes for the Gelfling of the clan.

Though some do use metal swords and the like, Stonewood hunters and trappers prefer stone-tipped spears and even finely crafted stone daggers. Made by a community of highly skilled woodcrafters, Stonewood spears are renowned for their durability and perfect balance.

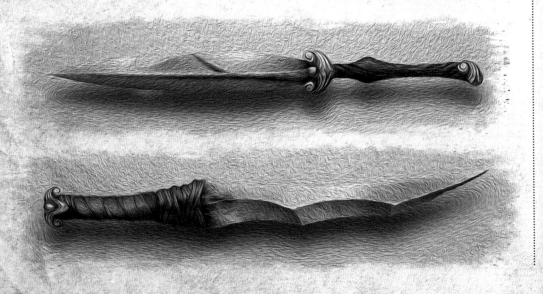

Gelfling Fire
and the Crucible

An incredible monument sits at the base of Bolentor. This is the Crucible and the Stonewood hearth.

The Crucible, like all Gelfling hearths, is the gathering place for the Stonewood during important occasions. This is the place where our maudra delivers announcements and conducts ceremonies, where newborns are introduced to the rest of the clan, and where traders from other regions are first greeted and welcomed to Stone-in-the-Wood.

Among these many communal purposes, one tradition that revolves around the Crucible is of particular note. Looking upon the hearth, one will find that the metal in the center of it—melted nearly beyond recognition—bears the form, here and there, of weapons.

It is this way by intent. Every time the Stonewood must take up arms, when the battle is over, the warriors carry their weapons to the Crucible. There dozens of swords and spearheads are jumbled upon one another and melted in the fires until they are no longer the instruments of violence they once were. Through this ritual, we separate our aggressive acts and memories from our everyday lives, leaving them to be consumed by the flames in the Crucible's belly.

The Crucible and this ritual of destruction by fire is a prime example of our relationship with our patron element: fire. It is said in many songs of ancient lore that when the Gelfling were split into seven clans, it was by way of the seven elements. Those with fire in their hearts, whose embers never die, became Stonewood. Our warmth lights and leads the way for other Gelfling, so much so that Stone-in-the-Wood is often regarded as the hearth of the seven clans—not only because of its central location, but also because of the bright, brave souls that inhabit it.

Many songs tell of a sacred place where, in the far future, the Gelfling will once again receive the blessing of Thra in the form of song; many of the far-dreamers who have peered into the flames and seen this dream believe that Stone-in-the-Wood may be the location foretold in the prophecies. After living beneath the mysterious stones of Bolentor and among my fellow proud and enduring Gelfling, I do not doubt this could one day become that place. For we Gelfling always gather at the hearth; and there is no greater hearth than Stone-in-the-Wood—in the shadow of Bolentor, where the flames of the Crucible grow steadily stronger upon the backs of melted swords!

ATTITUDE TOWARD OTHERS

Thanks to its location, Stone-in-the-Wood is a stop of necessity for any travelers on their way to nearly anywhere in the Skarith region. Although the Stonewood community benefits from this constant passage—often offering hospitality in trade for materials and produce from distant areas—the influx of outsiders has also reinforced many of the clannish mentalities inherent to Gelfling culture as a whole. While the Stonewood are friendly and welcoming to those passing through, we have also gone out of our way to preserve the privacy and strength of our internal community.

One of the most noticeable ways we have done this is by creating separate areas—way houses and wells, for example—for traveler use. Outsiders are welcome in these places, but should they wander mistakenly (or intentionally, I suppose) into other areas, they will be met with a very different reception. I am thankful for these places of privacy; as a youngling, I recall many times the village seemed full of outsiders. But they were not allowed to come to the place where I lived with my family, and so despite their ever-changing presence, I found stability and safety at home.

THE STONEWOOD LYRE

Among the Stonewood is one family who has made enchanted instruments for as long as any can remember; their craft is beyond impeccable, their work sought as far as the Citadel in Ha'rar by the All-Maudra's musicians. Of course, even as a youngling, I made sure to forge a strong relationship with these instrument makers. With their work being so popular, they were often busy or away collecting the materials necessary for their magnificent pieces, but they still made time for me whenever they could.

I still recall that fated day I was first invited into their workshop. I do not believe I have ever felt so close to divinity itself. Some may swear upon the Brothers or the Sisters. Some may worship the Skeksis. But this song teller is devoted to the magic of song and music, and as a youngling not even yet with wings, standing inside that workshop felt as if I were standing before the Crystal of Truth itself.

Over time I became more familiar to the workshop. I was invited to apprentice with them, though I sadly declined; my heart belongs to telling songs. Still I spent time there as they worked, practicing my reading and writing and singing. They built their pieces from powerful materials from all across Thra; contained in that small space were fragments of driftwood from the Silver Sea and stone from the Sifa Coast. Metals and woods and melted crystal sand. Shards of bone and hollow feathers. In that magical workshop, the Song of Thra resonated so strongly, I believe that any instrument made by those talented hands could have summoned the very voice of the Crystal in a single note.

FOOD

The culture of Stone-in-the-Wood is certainly one that favors the hunter-defender, a Gelfling archetype by which we Stonewood build our days and maintain our style of life. This is evidenced in many aspects of Stonewood traditions, though perhaps it is most readily illustrated in our relationship with the creatures that cohabit in the Endless Forest. While the Stonewood respect and value all life as much as any other clan, the forest is also one of the most dangerous regions of Thra. Eat or be eaten is the way of life there, regardless of how much one respects or values another.

And so, in this rich and competitive environment, the Stonewood rise to defend our homes and ourselves, and have developed sophisticated weaponry and armament to do so. This is the way of the hunter and the defender; one who knows the way of the cycle of life, prey and predator—one who uses this knowledge to protect oneself and the things one loves. This is not to say that Stonewood tradition does not abide by the laws of nature. We never hunt for sport. The Stonewood *staba-senta*—"wood watchers"—are keenly aware of the balance of creatures within the wood. The Stonewood tradition is to use hunting to maintain and uphold the balance within their sphere, not disrupt it.

Stonewood meals are traditionally served in groups around the hearth, and thus fire-roasting, baking, and searing are common ways in which dishes are prepared. The scent of clean smoke and food on the fire is always enough to make one's mouth water. Paired with the tart flavors of forest fruits—in particular the peachberry and my favorite, the dangerous-to-obtain bluemouth fruit—and a cup of cold water from the Black River, Stonewood meals are jolly, hearty, and unforgettable.

RECREATIONAL POISONS
AND THE SCREAMING TREE

The Endless Forest is home to some of the most diverse creatures, flora and fauna alike, all of which have developed their own means of surviving in the endless cycle of the natural world. Many are poisonous, warning predators of their toxic bodies with bright colors and alarming noises and movements. Others protect themselves with deadly venoms, delivered by fang or claw or stinger.

The Stonewood, having lived in this natural sphere for ages, have developed a most interesting use for the more harmful substances found within the creatures of the wood. Although some can be fatal in even a small dose, there are others that our apothecaries have been able to alter—through fire or water or soil—and distill into potable liquids.

One of the more involved procedures for distilling such a substance is used for the fruit of the *arara* tree, more commonly called the screaming tree. This tree bears sweet fruits that dangle in large purple clusters. Normally, the fruits are edible and quite delicious; however, the tree has a fascinating defense against creatures that might otherwise strip the fruits before they have a chance to seed: When the tree senses danger, it emits a terrifying screaming sound (the mechanism of which is a mystery).

The scream itself is alarming enough to scare many predators away, but if that weren't enough, when the screams of the tree are heard by the fruits, they secrete a poisonous goo that coats the clusters. This slime is potent enough to kill smaller creatures, but for Gelfling, it is only enough to send one into a dreamlike daze. In even smaller quantities, however, it has a relaxing effect, and so Stonewood apothecaries have found a way to extract the substance in the controlled environment of their workshops. This is the procedure:

First, the tree is approached quietly by experienced harvesters, who remove the berries so stealthily that the tree never has a chance to unleash its horrifying-sounding defense. The berries are then brought back to the apothecary's workshop. There the inert berries are broken into small groups and placed in bowls of water. The apothecary—having perfected the sound over many trine—then screams softly into the bowls one at a time, in the perfect tone of the screaming tree. Reacting to the apothecary's voice, the berries release their defensive slime, which dissipates into the water. Later this is reduced to a more measurable substance, bottled, and traded.

SONGS OF THE STONEWOOD

Beware the Hunter

When I was very young, the songs I was told around the campfires were mostly those of heroic feats and creation myths. But as I grew older and stayed by the fire later into the night, I heard new songs, told for older children. I remember one night in particular, as we sat beside the fire with Old Ari, a diamond-eyed song teller of the most distinguished pedigree. He played a three-stringed lute, a band of Sifan bells around his ankle, which he tapped in rhythm as he told a song most chilling:

Be safe, my childling
As you calm your heart
Look not beyond the window
Out into the dark

Be safe, my little one
Close your heavy eyes
Think not of the monster out there
Wearing a bone disguise

Be safe, my sweetest darling
As you drift into a dream
Hear not the frantic heartbeats
Hear not the panicked scream

Be safe, my dearest treasure
Till you feel the morning's rays
Feel not the presence at the door
Nor the Hunter's burning gaze

Dozens of songs have been sung of this character, a demonic monster that prowls the Endless Forest. He has several names, as all villains do (Bone-Mask and the Four-Arm are others). But most agree that he is best known as the Hunter: a bloodthirsty creature and the only of his kind, who lives for the sport of chasing and devouring his prey whole. Of course, during my extensive wandering within the Endless Forest, I have never encountered any sign that such a monster is real. Yet the frightening songs told of his terrible presence still work wonders in preventing younglings from wandering into the wood alone at night.

Jarra-Jen

It should come as no surprise to any that Jarra-Jen, the Lightning Born, was of the Stonewood clan. It is said that after each and every one of his many adventures, Jarra-Jen would return to his home in Stone-in-the-Wood, his pack full of treasures and mouth full of stories of his most recent triumphs. The most exciting of his songs were dream-etched upon stone slabs and set atop the Bolentor rise. There they remain to this day, proof of his legendary adventures that made the Stonewood clan famous far and wide.

The following is a humorous childlings' song told often in spring when the Fizzgigs—the Stonewood's sigil creature—awaken from their winter hibernation. Many creatures in the wood burrow underground in the colder seasons, and no matter the warnings issued by their parents, young Gelfling cannot be stopped from digging through the leaves and brush with sticks. This song is often told as a first reminder that you might find yourself in a predicament should you awaken any ornery creatures—though the ending of the song usually results in unstoppable giggles and laughter. This song is a crowd-pleaser, especially with children, for obvious reasons; the sound effect near the end is often unique to the song teller who tells it, allowing one to leave one's personal signature on the well-known song in the most ridiculous way.

Jarra-Jen and the Fizzgig King

At the end of the winter in the trine before last
The Fizzgigs of the wood began to break fast
Howling and barking for the awakening spring
Yet sleeps the largest of all: the Fizzgig King

His body is naught but a mouth and a tail
Fur thick and dark, teeth spiny and pale
But his snores shake the forest from treetop to root
Then his ears twitch as a twig snaps under boot

Yea, here comes our hero, our brave Jarra-Jen
Traveled the whole world and back again
Cutting through Fizzgig wood on his way back home
Boots heavy with soil and sand and sea foam

Our hero was tired and his tread was not quiet
As his path took him through the spring Fizzgig riot
'Twas all yipping and yapping along that forest trail
Jarra-Jen chuckled and waved. And then stepped on a . . .
tail?

RAWRRRRRRR!
The Fizzgig King had been snoring
But now he was awake and roaring!
His mouth opened huge and red and wide
With a giant gulp he sucked Jarra-Jen inside!

Aaaaaghhhhhh!
No one could hear Jarra-Jen's shout
"I'm terribly sorry, now please let me out!"
But the King was not in an agreeable mood
Jarra-Jen had to escape before he became food

To escape the huge maw was no easy feat
So Jarra-Jen tickled the King's throat with a leaf
And when the King wouldn't burp for his part
Jarra-Jen tickled backward and the King gave a loud

PPPPBBBBBBBBBBBBBBTTTTT!
Ah, fresh air at last!

And that is the tale that the song tellers sing
Of Jarra-Jen in the maw of the Fizzgig King

Bolentor, Pride of Stone-in-the-Wood

Of course, one cannot discuss Stone-in-the-Wood without making some remark of the stone rise around which the village is positioned. Though it may seem like an ordinary, natural geographical feature, closer inspection of the stones has led many rock readers to believe the boulders were moved from a variety of different locales. For example, there are some stones with a red hue found only among the Claw Mountains, far to the west, across the Crystal

Desert. Some of the boulders in the center of the rise are of a black, almost pitch color, and very dense—potentially from within the Grottan Mountains. And yet they are all overgrown with moss and trees and roots, some of which must be hundreds of trine in their own right.

It is not known how Bolentor, the stone rise that gives Stone-in-the-Wood its name, came to be, and every song teller seems to have their own story. Some told me a song of a giant that moved many stones from every corner of Thra to this place, so marking it as the center of the world. Some told me that the earth opened one day and the stones spilled out. Others said that the massive pile of stones was the droppings of an enormous bird.

My favorite song told of an unnamed Gelfling who sang with a voice so lonely and sad that the mountains to the east gave up their children. The stones tumbled down the cliffs and came to this place, and once arrived, there they stayed. Though her name is not part of the song, most Stonewood agree that this young Gelfling was Maudra Melyff, one of the first recorded maudras of Stone-in-the-Wood. Although we do not know the origins of this song, the consistency with which it is associated with Maudra Melyff is so strong that the legend is named after her.

Maudra Melyff the Rock Singer

Comes a young Gelfling through the green
Dark hair, dark eyes, and a voice pristine
Lays eyes upon the prettiest clearing she'd ever seen
Emerald grass, dancing trees, still lake between

Sits in the center, eyes closing, she meditates
On the wood and the earth and the gentle lake
Feels in her heart a most yearning ache
Lets out her voice, and the earth quakes

Sings her song of loneliness and pain
So sad and pure that the sky begins to rain
Cries out her soul in a yearning refrain
Till the east rockies shudder in twain

The mother of the mountains had heard her cries
Sent her children stones down from her heights
Tumbled to the clearing and now there they lie:
Maudra Melyff's Bolentor, the great stone rise

The Black River

The most prominent artery within the Skarith Basin, the Black River originates within the Grottan Mountains and empties into the Silver Sea at the port of Ha'rar, far to the north. Between those points, it twists through the Endless Forest, bringing crystal-clear water down from the mountains. Slow and steady, the river is ideal for transporting goods north to Ha'rar. Its banks are even and clear, making travel alongside its sparkling black waters easy for any wayfinder, novice or experienced.

Stone-in-the-Wood rests roughly midway between the Black River's spring and delta. The Stonewood Gelfling benefit not only from the river's clean and consistent water supply, but also from the wildlife that flourishes near the river. Thus there are hundreds of odes to the Black River from many song tellers inspired by its slow-moving waters—to tell them all would fill far too many scrolls. Instead, I have selected one from a Spriton trader who wrote this while visiting Stone-in-the-Wood and sang it before the Crucible as a thank-you to her hosts.

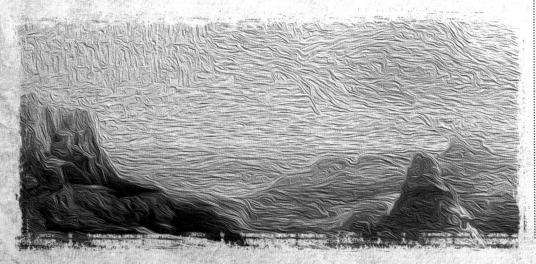

Black and Shining River (Spriton Origin)

O black and shining river
Night within the day of the wood
Wherever round you wander
Life rises from you, green and good

O black and shining river
Fated lifeline of the land
Telling all her quiet secrets
As a crease read in a gentle hand

O black and shining river
Wide from the forest to the sea
Guide me through the darkest night
Be my nighttime eyes so I can see

O black and shining river
Now take me out to sea
Though it was along your watery way
That I was ever truly free

Olyeka-Staba, the Cradle Tree

A walk's distance from Stone-in-the-Wood—if one knows the way—is a tree that towers above the others, its trunk as wide as the Black River. There is something so soothing about standing under the tree's impressive body; it has the same feeling as lying in the arms of one's mother and feeling the rest of the world fade away. It is no wonder, then, that the tree is called Olyeka-Staba, the Cradle Tree.

While the songs do not agree on how the tree came to be planted, most songs agree that the Cradle Tree is the origin of every tree in the Endless Forest. What the forest hears, the tree hears. What the tree feels, the forest feels. Stonewood Gelfling have gone to the Cradle Tree for hundreds of trine to sit beneath its dense emerald leaves, in the hopes of hearing its wisdom. Others visit to inspect the tree for illness, as a way to determine the health of the entire forest. And so it has been between the Stonewood and the Cradle Tree for as long as any song teller remembers.

The following is a song told by parents to their childlings as they rock them to sleep.

The Cradle Tree's Lullaby

Rest, my babe, as a flower in the shade
Close up your petals, hide your face away
Nestle in my arms as you fall asleep
Listening to whispers of your Cradle Tree

A Final Word

I left my clan in Stone-in-the-Wood on a sunny morning, eager to set out before I fully woke and realized the permanence of my decision. It was not natural to me, as a Stonewood, to leave and open myself to the whims of Thra and the other Gelfling living alongside us. The Stonewood way is to remain put, like the stones of the rise, and grow firm and strong. To become one with the earth and the fire, to prosper and to take pride in what one has made.

And so I knew I had to leave all at once or not at all. Had to send the sturdy stone rolling down the hill, to land where it may.

I looked back only once to bid farewell to my beloved Bolentor. As I did, I caught tears in my eyes. Even then, some part of me knew that although I could always return to the safety of the wood and the friendly faces that waited for me in their shell-and-stone homes, it would not be the same. For at the very least, I would be changed by what I planned to do—else why heed the call of Thra at all?

THE SPRITON CLAN

Spriton Plains

The Spriton Plains are a collection of rolling, gentle hills and meadows south of the Endless Forest. Their golden-green softness undulates like a sea of grass and wildflowers, rife with creatures big and small, scurrying below in burrows and loping above on long, thin legs. Within each valley are copses of trees gathered around brooks and streams, and in one such wood hides a collection of thatch-roofed Gelfling houses built around a central hearth. This is Sami Thicket, the home of the Spriton clan.

The Spriton are a medium-size Gelfling community with some hundred families cohabiting within Sami Thicket and the surrounding area. While most of the Gelfling in the clan live in the homes that circle their hearth and the Pavilion, I also found dozens of homes dotting the hills and fields beyond the wood. These smaller households are often groups of three to six family members, all of whom take part in cultivating the land near their homestead. Produce is then brought into Sami Thicket, where the families are received warmly by the rest of their clan.

The Spriton have the reputation of being territorial and, in some cases, aggressive and combative. However, I found in my experience this was more talk than truth. Although they have some rivalry with their neighbors—the Stonewood to the north and the Drenchen to the south—generally when Gelfling from beyond Sami Thicket came to visit (myself included), they were greeted politely and with respect. Keeping face is of great value among many Gelfling, of course, and the Spriton are not any different in this regard. In fact, most of the competitive attitudes I found were only among the youth, as one might find in any Gelfling community. Spriton younglings spend much

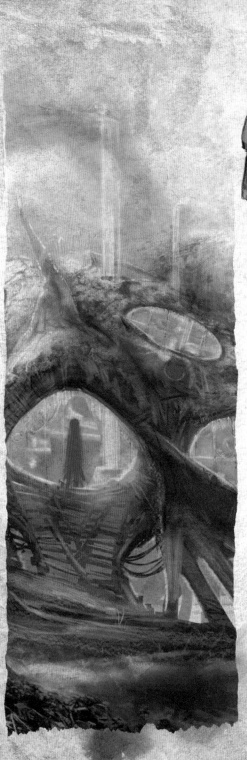

of their time refining their riding and hunting skills by participating in games of sport such as bola-throwing contests and knock-knee, a race-and-ball game played from the backs of Landstriders.

One of the most eye-opening things I learned during my time with the Spriton was how valuable generational knowledge is. This is true for any Gelfling community; however, the Spriton's agricultural livelihoods are largely based upon seasonal events—the trine cycle, of course, but also the greater seasons. The memory of one Gelfling is never as strong as that of many; thus, passing on the wisdom from previous generations becomes ever more important to ensure the success of the crops.

DAILY LIFE

The Spriton day begins with the suns rising and ends long after the sky grows dark. These long workdays are filled with the many tasks required to keep the Spriton community thriving. The Spriton have sorted their work into three categories, and as younglings grow into the age of apprenticeship, they are selected by mentors and begin training to participate in their work group of choice. Each group also has two elders who sit on the maudra's council.

The first group are the hearth workers, whose daily tasks are integrated in the care of the hearth and home. This group includes the caregivers as well as the woodworkers who build and maintain the physical homes in which the Spriton live—and also the song tellers who stoke the flames of the Spriton's spirits and hearts. Finally, the hearth workers also include the weavers, stitchers, and other artisans. Fine crafts and their creation are integral to the Spriton community, as interwoven with the clan's way of life as the thousand threads of a tapestry.

The second group are the dirt workers, who protect the land and cultivate the many gardens both within the thicket as well as in the nearby fields. Dirt workers keep the oral records of the seasonal wisdom, mark the passing of time upon the sun-sticks posted in the fields, and are equipped with horticultural and agricultural knowledge of countless generations. Dirt workers also tend to the creatures of the surrounding area, including lowland Fizzgigs and Landstriders, keeping track of their numbers and health, and thus, the health of the land.

The third and last group are the path workers. These Gelfling are responsible for preparing, sorting, counting, and trading the many Spriton products. From the fruits of the gardens to sandals, the path workers are strong with numbers and counting, and are well journeyed beyond Sami Thicket and the surrounding area. They are an adventurous, outgoing bunch with sharp tongues and charismatic smiles. There is a saying, "smooth as a Spriton wagon driver," which certainly finds its roots in these friendly, intelligent folk.

SPRITON CRAFT

Spriton magic crafts range from woven textiles and quilts to functional items such as spades, hoes, and even weapons—though their metalwork is not as refined as that of the Stonewood or Vapra due to the dearth of materials. Instead, the Spriton work mainly in charmed wood and fiber, and they are experts at using spells to bind substances of both vegetable and animal sources. Spriton wool, spun from the shed undercoats of various plains creatures, is a widely sought commodity, especially after taking dye from one of the hundreds of pigments made within Sami Thicket.

Spriton textiles are easy to spot, with their extensive variety of magic-enhanced colors, visible stitchwork, and embroidery; these elaborate and magnificent pieces are desired even by the Vapra of Ha'rar. Needlework is a talent highly valued within the Spriton community, as it symbolizes how the Spriton view themselves as "stitchers" of the Gelfling clans through their well-developed trade relationships.

Spriton sandals are particularly famous, and a prime example of how the Spriton transform their powerful commitment to their role among the Gelfling into an item that is sought by Gelfling far and wide. Aside from the sandals' inexhaustible soles, made from wood and leather, the straps and coverings feature intricate exposed threadwork. While sitting with a circle of sandal-making hearth workers, I learned that Spriton stitchers intentionally expose the threadwork on their garments and shoes instead of hiding it between the seams. The reason is that the sinews that bind the sandals are the most crucial element of any shoe. Without them, the sandal would fall apart, no matter how beautiful the coverings or durable the soles. Exposing the stitchwork highlights and respects it, instead of burying it within the shoe or seams.

Another example of this can be found in Spriton pottery. To make the clay more durable, Spriton potters often add tangle-weed to their mixture. This is not a process unique to the Spriton; many Gelfling fortify their clay with vegetation. However, when sculpting, the additives are encouraged toward the interior of the clay, or painted over after curing. It is not so with Spriton pottery. Instead, Spriton potters encourage the tangle-weed—often dyed and bespelled with beautiful, vibrant colors—to surface on the exterior of pots. In this way, like with the stitching, the strength of the clay is visible to all who gaze upon it.

Finally, the Spriton are superb instrument crafters. I have already shared my story of the instrument makers in my home of Stone-in-the-Wood; and although their skill was miraculous seeming, I must admit they may have rivals among the Spriton. I do not say this lightly, and only after having seen a Spriton lyre.

Most Gelfling lyres, as you know, have six strings, made from various materials, depending on the availability of natural sources. The Spriton lyre, however, has a seventh string, spun of Vapran metal mined from the mountains near Ha'rar. This seventh string is a mystery to me, though I have played the lyre since I was old enough to hold one; but in the hands of its maker, this lyre came to life with such sublime character, I cannot deny I was listening to the voice of Thra itself.

Cohabiting with Podlings

An interesting feature I noted in my time with the Spriton is that, while many Gelfling communities are populated only by Gelfling, the busy life in Sami Thicket is much more diverse. Landstriders wander through the Pavilion, Swoothu flit through the skies bearing messages from neighboring friends, and wild Windsifters make their nests among the trees. Even more remarkable to me were the number of Podlings who not only partake in daily life in Sami Thicket but have also built homes nestled between the Gelfling buildings and in the fields surrounding the thicket.

Podlings have always happily coexisted with Gelfling, whether in the Spriton lands or beyond, of course. I was delighted to see how seamlessly the Podlings were integrated among the Spriton, sharing in everything from farming tasks where the Gelfling and Podlings worked side by side all the way to a boisterous nursery of young Podlings and Gelfling, minded by a stern Podling mauddy.

Many Gelfling have learned the Podling tongue, and most Podlings can speak a bit of ours. I myself have studied several dialects of Podling and was able to have many a warm conversation with the Podlings who live among the Spriton. It was clear to me that the arrangement is one not of necessity but of enthusiasm; the Podlings and Spriton truly care for one another, and with great loyalty and joy call Sami Thicket their collective home.

THE PAVILION

At the center of Sami Thicket is the Spriton Pavilion, a clearing that radiates out from the stone hearth at its core. The Pavilion is a wonder to behold, paved with multicolored stones in red and gray and blue, arranged in a complex mosaic that resembles the twisting branches of a tree intertwined with a river. The hearth itself is ringed with a stone ledge wide enough for several Gelfling to stand on, or in the evenings when music is played, for a band to use as a stage.

Here in the Pavilion, the Spriton gather as a community, both on a daily basis to perform tasks that require large amounts of space (such as tanning leather or tending to the Landstriders' hooves) as well as to observe special events and occasions. The Pavilion is large enough that all the Spriton, including those who do not live within Sami Thicket, can gather. There is even room for the many Podlings.

Supper is also served at the hearth every evening for any who wish to attend. Hearth workers prepare these meals alongside the dirt workers who provide the food, either fresh crops or pickled produce and tubers, depending on the season. Fire keepers manage the firepit, which is large enough that it usually contains several smaller fires, though on special occasions, felled timber is brought in by wagon and a single fire is lit. When this happens, the flames tower above the village, lighting the entire Pavilion in the night as brightly as if it were day.

PATRONS OF THE LANDSTRIDER

The Spriton take the Landstrider as their sigil, honoring its noble disposition, fearlessness, and endurance. During my time with the Spriton, I had the opportunity to climb into the saddle with a few expert riders. These saddles are worn happily by the Landstriders, who are treated to fruit and nectar—their favorite meals—for wearing them and accommodating the riders. Many Landstriders are so accustomed to Gelfling riders, in fact, that they whistle and chirp at any Gelfling they see in hopes of exchanging a ride for a delicious snack.

As everyone knows, Landstriders are large creatures and uncomfortable in small spaces (though they do move with surprising stealth and speed through dense forest). While the Spriton care for several large herds of Landstriders at a time, most of this interaction takes place in the valleys outside Sami Thicket, where the earth slopes into 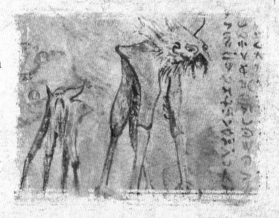 several grassy pockets where the Landstriders feel at ease. Here the Spriton have built a few structures to house Landstrider saddles and riding gear, and have erected feeding troughs and dug trenches to bend nearby rivers into the area for fresh water. The Landstriders come and go as they please, though in my experience, many of them find living in the valleys a peaceful and easy life—if there were a place I could go where I was fed and watered and groomed, I might prefer to remain there, too!

Riding is not as easy as it looks from afar. The saddles are made for standing in, with many straps that can easily entangle a novice rider—and the gait! With such long limbs, the Landstrider's lope can be jaw-jarring for the uninitiated. I am grateful for the experience, and more grateful still that my sore behind finally recovered, even if it took a few too many days to do so!

Despite spending only a moment in the saddle myself, I still learned much about Landstrider riding by listening to the riders. One thing I found most fascinating is that the Landstriders' most developed sense is their hearing, thanks to their enormous, sensitive ears. This allows the Landstriders to travel as easily at night as during the day: Although their eyesight is poor, they are able to listen to the echoes of their hoofbeats to "see" even at night—not unlike the Hollerbats native to the lightless Caves of Grot. Despite this remarkable ability, however, no Gelfling I asked would recommend the Landstrider as a steed for any nighttime adventure requiring stealth. Their heavy, ungainly bodies can be seen and their loud hoofbeats can be heard from far away.

Festival of the Sour Squash

Every autumn, the Spriton harvest the sour squash, a fruit of the earth that grows happily in the partial shade of the thicket. The squashes grow from yellow flowers, with thick flesh and rows of black pips along the center that are delicious when roasted. When the flowers are pollinated and transform into their bulbous squash form, they change slowly from green to an amber color. Finally, as they become ripe, they turn bright red. The ripeness of the squash marks the beginning of the harvest season and the coming of winter.

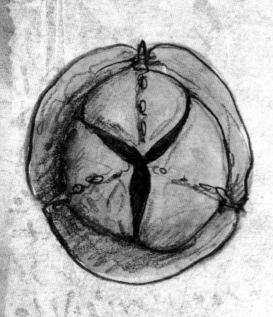

The Festival of the Sour Squash begins with the harvesting of the fruit and the gathering of the entire clan at the hearth. Younglings are given roasting poles heavy with squash, which they roast over the fire until the entire Pavilion is foggy with the sweet-scented smoke. The skin of the squashes grows crispy and flavorful, the inside warm and juicy. Their flavor matches their name; when raw, the sourness of the squash is almost unbearable. However, the roasting brings out a heady sweetness. If I could live on roasted sour squash alone, I would.

The festival celebrates the bounty of the harvest, giving thanks to Thra for its generosity. And so, it is considered very bad luck to decline to share. The roasted squashes are shared with the Podlings, of course, as well as any other creatures attracted by the scent. The tradition is that you must only give the squashes you roast. It is not until one is given to you that you may eat. In their eagerness, younglings with stomachs a-growling run with poles and squash, trying to deliver as many of the fruits as possible in the hopes of being gifted their first of the season in return. They do often discover that the joy of delivering the squash becomes its own reward.

Life Beyond Sami Thicket

Though most do, many Spriton do not live within Sami Thicket. This was a surprise to me, both because it is generally uncommon for Gelfling to live far from their maudra and hearth, and also because of the Spriton's belief in community and clan above all else. Despite these truths, almost an entire third of the Spriton clan lives in small homesteads built beyond the wood of Sami Thicket—some a distance of more than a day's journey.

When I asked the maudra about this and its effect on the community, she suggested I see for myself. She introduced me to a farmer who was visiting to deliver his crops and asked if he would take me with him. He did, and the following morning we left Sami Thicket together. It took the better part of the day to reach his homestead, built of sturdy logs atop a little hill. There he lived with his partner and their children, as well as his elderly mother. The hill sprawled with their sour squash patch and other crops; the sky was open and blue, with no other Gelfling in sight. The evening we arrived, we ate before their cookstove as his children told him songs of their adventures since he'd been gone.

The answer to my question was simple: The Spriton who live beyond Sami Thicket are as much a part of their clan as those who live within it. I felt no disconnect between the family that lived on the hill and the maudra waiting for them back in the Pavilion. Should they have needed anything, their clan would have provided; in return, they brought vegetables and timber once an unum to provide for the others. And of course, when the entire family made the journey—on special occasions, or just for the practice of traveling—they always arrived to the Sami Thicket Pavilion to a warm and happy reception.

Could this be the future of Gelfling life? As our clans grow and spread, certainly we cannot always remain as secluded as we are now. At one time, it frightened me to imagine living out of sight of Stone-in-the-Wood's Bolentor. But after spending some days with the Spriton family, and never once feeling alone or afraid, I wonder now what it might be like to, when I retire, take up a place within the Endless Forest. At home within the forest that is so much broader than the glade where my hometown rests. Would I still feel connected to my maudra? My family? My clan?

That night I sat on the stoop with the Spriton family, watching the suns set across the gentle plains. I felt for the first time that we were all connected, regardless of distance. It is not a single place that holds us together, but a collection of places, all within the same tapestry. Is that tapestry then merely a map of Thra? Or is it something that transcends geography itself? To this question I still have no answer, even after my many travels.

SWOOTHU TRAINING

Swoothu and Windsifters are both creatures that can be trained to carry messages and items over long distances. However, the two have very different strengths; while a Windsifter may reach its destination much more quickly and without fail, they are more aloof, preferring to heed the Song of Thra rather than fulfill more mundane tasks set forth by Gelfling.

Swoothu, as an alternative, are slightly more convincible creatures motivated by food and shelter. They are able to understand some aspects of Gelfling speech, as well as able to remember multiple destination requests. In addition, they are bigger than Windsifters and can carry more than small items or a single letter. This added bulk means Swoothu are slower and can sometimes take unum to arrive; however, many Gelfling prefer them to Windsifters because of their generally amiable dispositions.

The training of Swoothu is something in which Spriton dirt workers excel. Swoothu nests are built throughout the wood of Sami Thicket, allowing the winged creatures to rest after their long journeys, as well as eat, drink, find a mate, and raise offspring, all in the protected safety of the thicket. The Swoothu prefer covered dens high in the trees; in the wild they build such nests from mud and sticks. The Spriton-built dens are crafted from twine, clay, and sanded board, filled with hay and other bedding, which the Swoothu seem to enjoy immensely.

For training, Spriton work alongside several Swoothu at once, teaching them Gelfling language commands in exchange for morsels of roasted fruit. The Swoothu will do almost anything for the treats, flying in complex patterns on their transparent, buzzing wings. The process teaches the Swoothu that Gelfling can be trusted and, perhaps more importantly, the benefit of living among them. As the Swoothu grow older, their adoration of their Gelfling partners is exhibited in frequent visits, even when no messages are being delivered.

When Swoothu are ready to begin their work flying between major Gelfling locations—namely Stone-in-the-Wood, the Castle of the Crystal, Sami Thicket, and Ha'rar—they accompany Spriton traders on their voyages. The choice to depart is always left to the Swoothu. Many young Swoothu are fearful of the area beyond the thicket, but there comes a time when their curiosity exceeds their caution. Many Swoothu will travel with their Spriton hosts for unum before they are ready to make the journeys on their own.

FOOD

The Spriton's long tradition of agricultural wisdom is known by all the seven clans; most of the produce found in larger Gelfling villages originates from the Spriton's cleverly irrigated fields and robust crops. Thanks to countless generations perfecting the art of gardening and communing with Thra, the Spriton have developed ways to elongate growing seasons and yield bigger crops. They have even found methods of growing fruits and vegetables that do not normally grow in their region, whether due to climate or environment.

Due to the bounty of their agriculture practices, the Spriton's diet is traditionally heavy on fruit and vegetables. They rarely eat meat, and when they do, it is from a carefully chosen creature that is slaughtered swiftly and with great respect. Living in harmony with plants and creatures is a tenet of Spriton culture, possibly springing from the legend of the Six Sisters, a song that sings of the seven tasks assigned to the first maudra.

Spriton cuisine is often in the form of greens mixed with vegetables and fruits, sometimes marinated in a tangy sauce or seasoned with fire-toasted seeds or nuts. Although the Spriton rarely eat meat, their cheeses are a treasure of great variety, ranging from soft, spreadable kinds to those as hard as rocks and better suited to grating and melting. Such products are widely sought, and fetch good prices, especially in places like Ha'rar, where they are hard to come by.

SONGS OF THE SPRITON

Podling Song

I learned this sad lament from the Podlings who lived in a small hut beside the home of my hosts in Sami Thicket. Though the Podlings were normally lively and cheerful, during my time in Sami Thicket, one of the young Podlings was tragically caught unaware by a panicked Horner. It was a sad day indeed. His funeral was held in the Pavilion and attended by Podlings and Spriton alike; as his family prepared his body for burial, his father sang this song through his tears. I share it here along with a rough translation.

Podling Funeral Song

Tindyebo Bekna Staba doqa alori
Shyata-oyo zeshaba aduma doda avi
Yamda bi kiraba Vapa So shi
Dze Aslampia 'pida ya utomshi

Boka babi, yamda shoshi ashao
Ada bao temar mots nyotyano
"Yeta 'pida soraro?" bao temar'ashai
Aslampia shyayo adado vatai

"Apada arwe shi. Apadido dana
Aslam mala-ga sazaba ya Thra"

Within the Endless Forest I wandered
I met a creature dressed in bone white
Its eyes were bright like the Silver Sea
I knew it was Death come for me

I fell to my knees in front of him and cried
Still he didn't listen to my sad request
"Why me?" I asked in a tearful voice
He sighed before he replied

"I'm merely a servant performing my duty
It is Thra that is calling you home"

The Mysterious Shadows of Mystic Valley

Somewhat to the north, between Sami Thicket and the Endless Forest, is a natural ravine formed by a long-evaporated river. Here, the rumors go, many Gelfling have spotted strange figures, their spidery silhouettes cast long and dark against the golden walls of the valley. At night, the rumors sing, droning howls and chants echo from within like a chorus of wailing spirits.

Though I visited this place several times during my travels, I never sighted any of these mysterious figures myself. The valley itself is quite beautiful, flowing almost like a river and full of stones.

The wind called in strange refrains, rushing through the contours of the ravine, but I never heard the moaning voices. When the suns set, the trees that grow from the top of the ravine throw their shadows along the walls, stretching them in sometimes ominous proportions. But as much as I searched for the supernatural creature, or creatures, I did not find them. And, as far as I know from the tales of historians and other travelers, neither has anyone else.

Despite my personal experiences, I cannot deny the number of songs that have been written about the mysterious valley and its even more mysterious inhabitants. Some songs say the ravine is filled with the ghosts of a long-gone race. Others say it is where the Arathim now reside, and it is their many-armed bodies projecting the inky black shadows. Yet other songs claim the valley is the birthplace of the Hunter, the beast told of in many Spriton and Stonewood tales. My favorite version of this song is one that tells of the way in which the Hunter became such a bloodthirsty ghoul that he used a sharp rock to cut away his soul, rendering him without a heart. His disembodied spirit remains in the valley and moans for his body's return.

The Hunter's Knife

Creeping in the shadow valley, the Hunter walks in pain
His bloodlust overpowers him, his rage he can't contain
Yet even in his breast, a shriveled heart remains

And so he finds a sharpened rock and fashions him a knife
To stop the bleating of his heart every time he takes a life
To cut away the soul that cannot bear his destiny of strife

He strikes upon his shadow, wields the knife upon his soul
Crying tears of misery, longing to be un-whole
Then splits away his heart, leaving red a gaping hole

His severed spirit flickers weak, like light within a glass
Pain and sorrow, heart and soul, forevermore outcast
Through a grin of victory, the wicked Hunter laughs

"With this done, it's over now—from pain finally free
From one, two made! All split and rent asunder we
No longer whole, no longer us. Now, just you and me"

The Hunter runs and leaves him there, beating out in pain
Writhing with four wretched arms, miserably cleft in twain
Howling in the shadow valley, the Hunter's heart remains

Day of the Great Sun

Most Gelfling celebrate the Day of the Great Sun with traditional summer activities—carrying water, taking a day of rest, and the like. I learned that among the Spriton, who name this celebration Longest Day, this event is observed with what they call "sun filling." In the days leading up to Longest Day, the Spriton cut back the trees surrounding Sami Thicket and remove the thatching from their roofs so only the rafters remain. This way, when the Great Sun takes his longest journey across the sky, his light can fill the homes of the Spriton—enough, the hope is, to last the rest of the summer and through winter until the next trine.

During the course of Longest Day, any old or discarded items that have been cleaned out are gathered in the Spriton hearth and burned. The fire rages for the entire day, in effigy of that which is no longer needed or desired. Finally, homes sorted and dusted and filled with sun, the head of each household takes a small handful of ash from the hearth and sprinkles it atop their re-thatched roofs. In this way, the first coat of dust is a respectful reminder of the old.

Here is a song sung during sun filling, in particular when beating out heavy quilts and mats so they may be filled with sun instead of dust.

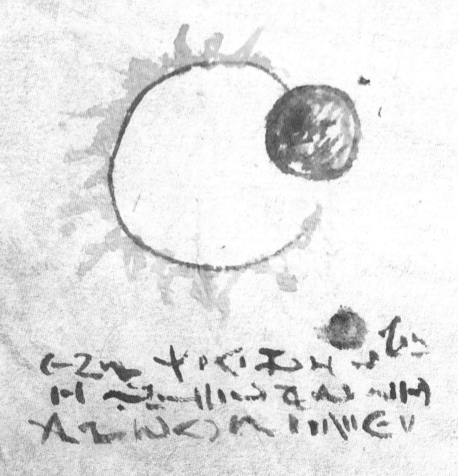

Sun-Filling Song

Hey-oh, aye-yo, hey
Blessed Longest Day
Yea-oh, hey-oh, yo
Gray burned up by gold

Fie-fey, hi-ho, fie
Grass of greenest green
Hi-ho, yea-hey, hi
Clearest bluest sky

Mun-yo, hi-ha, mun
Fill up with the sun
Hey-oh, aye-yo, hey
Blessed Longest Day

The Low Tree

Sami Thicket is a small wood with two hearts; one is the Spriton Pavilion, where the hearth and homes are. The other nexus is a short walk through the wood, where the ground dips lower toward a winding brook. At the bottom of this bowl-like valley is a squat tree with fat, bulging roots and thin, reedy branches ruffled with hand-shaped golden leaves. This is the Low Tree, the Spriton's patron tree. Its roots are as gnarled as Aughra's knuckles, rising above the ground so one can wander beneath in a maze of dangling roots and vines. Youngling Spriton play here, and elders meditate in its shade. Sami means "to rest"; I believe, after spending many days listening to the wind in its fragile leaves, that it is this tree that gives the thicket its everlasting name.

Ode to the Low Tree

Come sleep beneath the swaying boughs
Of the Low Tree in the wood
Roots that bind the earth to stone
Of the Low Tree in the wood

Rest your head on her knee and dream
Oh, the Low Tree in the wood
Water drink up from the crystal stream
Oh, the Low Tree in the wood

Hear songs whispered within the leaves
Of the Low Tree in the wood
Proud maudra of the flower fields
Oh, the Low Tree in the wood

A Final Word

I ended my stay with the Spriton on a crisp autumn day, a pair of new farewell sandals on my feet and a pack full of dried squash and emroot. My Spriton friends walked me to the edge of Sami Thicket to say goodbye, leaving me with words of encouragement and wishes of good fortune. In my youth, I would have never expected such familial friendliness from our longtime rivals; as I left through the well-kept, peaceful fields where Spriton and Podlings worked side by side, I reflected on this singular change of heart, this small symptom of a greater change in me. That things are not always the way we expect them to be, and the only way to discover this is to walk among others with an open mind and heart.

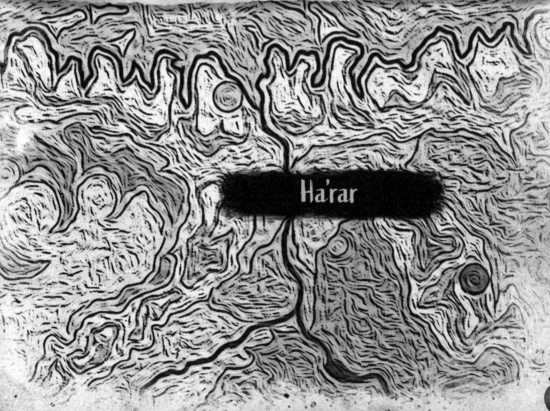

The Vapra Clan

Ha'rar

North of the Endless Forest, the Black River flows through Namopo Valley toward the northern shores. The land rises on either side of the river's neck into hard blue and gray mountains. The tallest peaks among the range are well above the place where the trees stop, eternally capped in white snow that shines, unmelting, even under the light of the suns.

Where the Black River meets the Silver Sea, the cliffs rise sharply on either side, covered by ice in the winter and kissed by mineral-green waves in the summer. There the domed, thatched roofs of Ha'rar cluster around the magnificent Vapran Citadel—home of the All-Maudra, and capital of the Gelfling world.

The Vapra are known in the Skarith Land for their elegant appearance and lifestyle, luxuries afforded to them by, and often displayed as proof of, their relationship with the Skeksis. Flowing garments and extravagant hairstyles are not uncommon, even among the Vapra who perform trade or menial work; jewelry of metals and gems is worn to signify prestige and wealth, so that the social hierarchy even within Ha'rar can be preserved. Similarly, the Vapra have taken on a particular way of speaking, which in some ways resembles the accent of some of the Skeksis Lords when they use the Gelfling tongue. This accent is distinct and noticeable, and the Vapra seem to enjoy emphasizing it when speaking with non-Vapran Gelfling or with the Skeksis themselves.

Despite their reputation, once I had spent more than a nominal amount of time in Ha'rar, I found that many of my preconceptions dissipated like snow melting in morning sun. Although some Vapra still treated me as an outsider, it was no more extreme than when I had visited any of the other clans, and in truth, the overwhelming majority of Vapra that I met were considerate, curious, and polite. Beyond that, I found their knowledge of history and the world in general to be quite worthy of my expectations. Thanks to their high literacy and wealth of written arcana, most Vapra have a thorough knowledge of the history of the Gelfling, the Skarith Land, the Skeksis, and many other topics. How they use this wisdom is left to them, of course.

DAILY LIFE

Life in Ha'rar is very different from life in other areas of the Skarith Land, and not just because of its chilly climate. Thanks to its location at the mouth of the Black River, the Vapra of Ha'rar enjoy a constant influx of merchants and goods. And, thanks to the All-Maudra's relationship with the Skeksis Lords, Ha'rar is a world of riches and luxury, where Gelfling are able to devote their time and energy to scholarly and political activities. Of the trade work performed by the Vapran artisans, colored glass and fine decorative metalwork are most famous; the stained glass windows in the rear of the All-Maudra's chambers—visible even from outside the Citadel—are one of the most magnificent artifacts in the modern Gelfling world.

The Gelfling of Ha'rar have very private lives, spending their days working in their trade, and their evenings at home with their families. Rather than all in the clan rising and working at the same time, the Vapra's schedules are self-determined based on their needs and the needs of the others who rely on them. This is effective for the large number of Vapra (and some other Gelfling) who make up the Ha'rar community; like a creature with many organs, the Vapra all do their part, together but specialized, and thus the community flourishes.

Due to their location so far north, the seasons of Ha'rar are slightly different from those of other areas where Gelfling dwell. The winters are long and dark, with snow falling nearly every day except on rare sunny days in summer. Although I am accustomed to cold winters, even I was caught off guard by the depth of the winters endured by the Vapra. On the last days nearing the solstice, the Great Sun's light shines for only a few moments, and on others not at all.

It is probably ignorant for me to belabor this phenomenon. The Vapra themselves, of course, think little of it; preparation for the darkness of winter is a recurring event, the shortening days at the end of summer a daily reminder. Yet I cannot help but see how walking on the shore between light and dark has made a lasting impact on these strong-willed Gelfling of the north. At the very least, it left its mark on me.

THE ROLE OF THE ALL-MAUDRA

Long ago, the seven clans were fraught with discord. We struggled with seemingly unsurmountable rivalries, constantly engaged in territorial skirmishes and dwelled on differences we thought we could not overcome. However, thanks to the Skeksis' vision and wisdom, we were able to find order. The Skeksis chose the Vapra to represent all clans in the Skeksis court, finalizing once and for all which clan's leader would be called All-Maudra from that day forward. From her throne in the Citadel, the Vapran All-Maudra heeds the Skeksis' will and brings it to the rest of the Gelfling. And in this way, we have order, and wisdom, and most importantly, peace.

The All-Maudra's throne

The All-Maudra bears a heavy burden, of course. The Skeksis are formidable and demanding and, for all their wisdom, understandably impatient with us mortal Gelfling. Unlike maudras of other clans, who are able to devote all their time to caring for their clan, the All-Maudra must divide her focus between the Vapra, the six other clans, and the Skeksis Lords. I believe this is one reason that the Gelfling of Ha'rar have come to self-regulate their daily tasks in such an organized fashion; without their individual responsibilities met, the livelihood of the city would be in jeopardy. It is very noble and respectable that as a community, they have come to an arrangement that allows the All-Maudra to fulfill her duties.

Another result of the All-Maudra's distance is that some Vapra may go their entire lives without ever having met her. This is—oh, how shall I put it?—*less traditional* than the role of maudras in other clans. The very word *maudra* means "mother"; among my home clan, for example, all Gelfling of the clan regard our maudra as a mother, second only to our birth mother. If a Gelfling's parents were ever unable to perform their caregiving duties, the maudra would adopt the child as her own. My maudra was there the day I was born, and there the day I climbed Bolentor and wrote my sigil on the top of the rise. I trust her as I trust no one else, and she knows me perhaps better than I know myself.

It is not the same with the All-Maudra, whose time is so divided. To merely gain a hearing with her is an exceptional honor. It is understandable why this is so, and yet I cannot shake the feeling that it is not right. When traveling among the seven clans, I have always done my best to keep an open mind and remember that other clans have different traditions from the ones I am accustomed to—all of which should be respected. And yet, this distancing of the maudra from her clan, even if it is so that she may serve the Skeksis Lords . . . although I understand it, in the privacy of these pages, I must confess that I do not like it at all.

THE TITHE

Once every three unum, the other clans make the journey to Ha'rar to join the Vapra in offering their goods to the Skeksis for the Vapran tithe. This ceremony is a tradition many Gelfling look forward to, as it offers one the rare opportunity to behold the Skeksis and the All-Maudra face-to-face. In a long procession that lasts several days, Gelfling present the products of their labor—be it grain or fruits of the harvest, handmade crafts and goods, or a particularly devoted song teller's tale— to the Skeksis in the hopes of winning favor for their family and their clan.

I had the opportunity to attend one tithe, and thanks to the rapport I had built among the All-Maudra's council in the time leading up to it, I had the immense honor of an invitation to behold the tithe from within the upper gallery of the All-Maudra's throne room. This was the only time during all my travels when I beheld the Skeksis Lords with my own eyes: the Collector, the Ritual Master, and the Scroll-Keeper attended. It is a memory that will be preserved within my heart and mind for all time. Their bejeweled robes, overflowing with fur and feathers; their tall figures draped in gowns of the richest colors and stitched with metallic thread. Unlike any creature of Thra, they overpowered every hall they walked, commanded the attention of every eye that opened. Even the All-Maudra seemed but a child in their presence.

One by one, small groups of Gelfling came before the Skeksis. There they knelt, offering their tithe in handwoven baskets or chests adorned with what decorations they could afford. But before the Skeksis, even the most elaborate Vapran trinket seemed like a child's toy; and what else could one expect? The Skeksis built the Castle of the Crystal; there they rule with only the Three Brothers above them, and even then, the suns seem but wanderers traveling along the paths ordained by the Skeksis Lords.

So what tithe could a Gelfling possibly offer that might suffice? Perhaps that is the purpose of the tithe, in reality—to humble the Gelfling and remind us of our limited comprehensions and narrow frames of mind. To remind us that we are but flowers in a garden tended by a much wiser, more powerful gardener than we could possibly understand. The tithe is not a tithe but a practice of humility—a sign of our acknowledgment of the Skeksis' sovereignty and an embodiment of our willing, needful prostration.

A NEW ALL-MAUDRA

Though not often, the time eventually does come when the ruling All-Maudra must pass on her position to an heir, usually her eldest daughter. When the date for the ceremony of appointing the new All-Maudra is set, the All-Maudra breaks her Living Crown into seven pieces. Six of the pieces are sent by Windsifter to the maudras of the other six clans, who then make the pilgrimage to Ha'rar with their piece of the crown. This gathering of the maudras with their eldest daughters and closest councils is a celebrated occasion, bringing Gelfling from all across the Skarith Land to Ha'rar to witness the event.

In a rite showing their loyalty to the Vapra and the All-Maudra, the six incumbent maudras reassemble the Living Crown and place it upon the brow of the new All-Maudra. Each imbues her piece with a blessing and an oath of fealty, not only to the All-Maudra, but also to what she represents as the Gelfling ambassador to the Skeksis. It is to announce their loyalty to the All-Maudra, to the Vapra, and to the Skeksis Lords, whom she represents. This has been the way since the Skeksis created the role of All-Maudra and ordained the Vapra the bearer of her duties.

CHRYSALISDAY—CELEBRATION OF THE SISTER MOONS

There is a night twice a trine on which all three moons appear in the sky (or so the stargazers say. I suppose we must trust them, for it is impossible for a Gelfling to see the Hidden Moon by eye alone, though I have heard from far-dreamers it is possible to feel it in one's heart), celebrated by Gelfling across the land as the Celebration of the Sister Moons.

In Ha'rar, this fated night is preceded by Chrysalisday, named for the chrysalis form of the Unamoth, the Vapra's sigil creature. Common in the north, Unamoths cover the trees like a coat of fluttering white petals. During the mating season, millions of Unamoths flock on the northern coasts, until every surface is flowing with their white and silver wings. They lay their eggs along the rocky mountain faces and the frozen bark of windward-facing trees, and when spring arrives, the eggs hatch into worms, which later go dormant inside their glowing chrysalises.

Herein lies the mystery of the Unamoth, which enchants even the wisest of Gelfling sages. For although Unamoths are common and easy to observe, no naturalist or far-dreamer has ever been able to predict when the Unamoth chrysalises will blossom, releasing newly transformed moths. Some of the chrysalises open within unum; some have been known to wait trine. Still others, kept as amulets of good luck, have never awakened—and perhaps never will. I have heard that the All-Maudra keeps many chrysalises within her personal chambers, as a reminder of the potential of the future and the unpredictability of fate.

And so, the Vapra, enamored with the mysteries of their Unamoths, begin the Celebration of the Sister Moons on Chrysalisday. On this day, the youth of the city carry lanterns along the streets down to the wharf. The procession and the release of the lanterns are intensely beautiful as the sky darkens and fills with flickering lights, rising quickly toward the Sisters as they hover over the sea.

The lanterns themselves are made of paper, crafted by hand by their bearers. In its pulp form, the paper is roughly mixed with flammable dust. These veins of bluedust eventually catch fire from the heat of the lantern's candle, exploding in a pop of color and light. However, thanks to the uneven distribution of the dust, it cannot always be predicted when such a thing will occur, if at all. Thus, the release of the lanterns is symbolic of the unpredictable transformation of the Unamoth as it escapes from its chrysalis, fluttering off into the night in a spark of color and light.

THE ART OF FLIGHT

It is no secret that the Vapra, whose wings are broad and light, are masters of flight; in competition, they are rivaled only by the Sifa from a purely physical perspective. But what I did not know until I arrived in Ha'rar was how the Vapra's homeland encourages their ability in the air as well. Wind is constantly blowing in from the Silver Sea, striking the cliffs upon which Ha'rar sits and gusting upward and through the area at all times. Hot springs riddle the mountains, and several springs flow down underground channels beneath Ha'rar and nearby areas. Within the village, jets of steam explode from vents carved for that purpose, mimicking the geysers and natural escape holes that occur naturally in the rugged mountains.

These hundreds of invisible, airy pathways crisscross through this land characterized by mountain heights; all one must do to ride them is spread one's wings. So reliable are these currents that many homes have additional doorways on the roofs, adorned with sculpted hand- and foot-rails and platforms for comfortable landings. It is no wonder that the Vapra have been able to refine their abilities in the air and on the wing so well, with such ample opportunities to be airborne so easily.

Even still, not all of the Vapra's aerial prowess can be credited to their environment. Hand-in-hand with their location and its natural benefits is the Vapran tradition of flight; as far back as any Vapra can remember, taking wing has been one of the most joyous pleasures of Gelfling life. And it is not just for recreation. Perhaps most importantly within Ha'rar, flight is a sign of ability, prestige, and power. Disputes between women are settled in the air in tests of agility and strength; many Vapran garments made for men include wing-shaped vestments along the back. I heard more than once among the Vapra that their (self-proclaimed) superior skills in flight are the reason the Skeksis selected them to lead the Gelfling through the All-Maudra.

THE HA'RAR PORT MARKET

I spent many of my days in Ha'rar wandering the market. Thanks to the ever-changing tides and Gelfling, every day is new and fresh with sights and sounds and scents. Song tellers play for stories and word from distant places; merchants trade and barter; carpenters and stoneworkers repair ships; and healers mend wounds. Here you can find anything you might be looking for, so long as you have goods to trade, from Vapran steel and Grottan poultices to the whispers of a far-dreamer whose cryptic visions may hold the key to your very future.

When the winds favor it, the Sifa arrive in the Ha'rar port in fleets, their bright ships bringing a shock of color to the usually monochrome sea. Spriton set up their carts alongside Stonewood; I even spied Dousan and Drenchen travelers on occasion. It is a place where Gelfling of nearly every walk of life convene,

soldiers from the castle among farmers from the Spriton Plains, all together in one place for a common goal. The only other location I can imagine may be similar is the Castle of the Crystal, where Gelfling from all seven clans unite to serve the Skeksis.

I had once thought it impossible for so many Gelfling of different clans to exist together in peace. But the market, though boisterous and busy, was an example that such a thing is not beyond us, despite what we may think. Could this place be the future of the Gelfling? As the wealth and prestige of the Vapra grows, could the bounds of the city spread? Might the trade routes along the Black River encourage more Gelfling to travel north—or may the Sifa perhaps adopt the design of the Dousan's skiffs and ride the river south? Could it be possible, one day, for the seven clans to truly coexist? Though far off it may be, I found myself drawn to the market for this taste of our potential future. Perhaps one day I will summon the courage to ask a far-dreamer.

Mountain Hot Springs

Though I have mentioned before the way in which the Vapra express their status by way of ornaments and elaborate modes of dress, I would be remiss if I did not balance this with a description of my most interesting experience among the mountain's hot springs. These springs, pools of hot green water that bubbles up from deep below the mountains, pocket the blustery cliffs in steamy groves. The hot springs are a difficult destination—though the reward is surely worth the dangers of the mountain climb.

I was able to reach just one of the springs, and only with the help of an experienced guide. Through freezing wind and constant blizzards we climbed; I slipped and nearly fell to my death a hundred times. On the trail we passed no one, bundled in our silver cloaks as my eyelashes froze. Every step was more challenging than the last, and with nearly every breath I considered turning back.

But then the wind broke. In the sudden stillness my vision cleared and my senses returned; I smelled the pure water and saw that a dozen Vapra lounged within the pools. My guide sternly instructed me to disrobe before entering the vicinity of the pools. There in the springs, he explained, all Vapra are one—nay, all Gelfling, for there were others like myself who had made the journey, though they were not of Vapran descent.

Stripped of our material garments, hair teased from braids and unadorned with any jewels or metals, I could not tell whether my companions in the springs were merchants, song tellers, elders, or the All-Maudra's daughters themselves. Equalized in our Gelfling skins, held in the soothing palm of the mountains, we reflected together: upon the fragility of our lives amid the raging snowstorm; upon the healing waters sent up from the belly of Thra; upon the dichotomy of warmth and cold represented by the springs themselves. Though I might not have believed it in the beginning, I found in the springs that the Vapra do, in fact, have the same natural drive as any other Gelfling: to find peace and balance, and to become one with Thra.

FOOD

Thanks to their position both as a port and as the Gelfling capital, the Vapra enjoy foods brought for trade from across the entire Skarith region. Sifan and Grottan spices abound at the wharf market, their scents mingling with those of fresh fish, ripe fruit, and meats from the woods and fields to the south. If you have a craving for a food of nearly any kind, you are likely to find it close at hand in Ha'rar—though depending on the source, you may be asked to pay handsomely for it.

When I first arrived in Ha'rar, I was dazzled by the array of cuisines available. After my many travels, I found it fascinating to see how the Vapra prepared many meals that are traditional dishes of other clans. The Vapra have what I feel is a more hesitant approach, using fewer spices and preferring less seasoning in general. However, Vapran cuisine tends to be sweeter than other dishes, perhaps thanks to the groves of sugarwood that thrive in the wintry climates and high altitudes.

After a time enjoying the reinvented cuisine of Ha'rar, I sought out a traditional chef who might be able to prepare for me something that is unique to the Vapra way of life. After a long search I finally ended up in the kitchens of the Citadel. The head chef there has been serving the All-Maudra and her family for many trine, and was trained by his parents, who were trained by their parents before them. I asked if he might prepare for me the most traditional Vapran dish he could imagine.

He did not disappoint. A hearty, sweet stew of mushrooms and cream was the main course, served with a baked mint-apple over top of it and garnished with shimmering Hooyim oil. After supper he brought me a slice of Vapran frost— soft cheese dusted in powdered sugar. It was simply divine.

Songs of the Vapra

The Citadel and Legacy of the All-Maudra

The Citadel of the All-Maudra is a legendary landmark, visible from nearly anywhere along the coast and most certainly the highlight of any visit to Ha'rar. The Citadel is built from stone carved from the Vapran mountains, reinforced with crystal and metal. The windows are made of stained glass in rainbow colors, shaped in the likeness of wings. The interior architecture resembles that of a whorled white shell, or perhaps a wave-smoothed stone; I could walk for days within the halls and never tire of their smooth stone speckled with tiny shards of crystal that glitter like fresh snow.

Who built the Citadel, and when, are facts lost to time and now transformed into legend; however, most historians assume that the Citadel was built by the Vapra with the help of the Skeksis and their infinite wisdom. When I walked among its silvery, sunlit halls, it was difficult to believe otherwise. It is a structure unparalleled in beauty and importance, an obelisk built to honor the Vapra's loyalty to the Skeksis Lords.

It is the symbol of the Vapra, the home of the All-Maudra, and certainly the most impressive Gelfling architectural feat of our time.

One boastful ditty—meant to be humorous, I think, in an effort not to be utter blasphemy—goes so far as to compare the Citadel to the Skeksis' Castle of the Crystal:

Twin Castles

One dark and one light
Black obsidian and silver ice
Lovely crowns of equal height
In this world exist but twice

Not all Gelfling revere the Citadel as highly as this. Wandering within the Citadel, I first heard a different song from an old woman while she swept. Day after day I returned, listening as she swept the halls and sang this song in her gentle, even voice. It struck me as beautiful, in its mundane way; perhaps an echo of how things were long ago, before the Citadel and the Skeksis and the All-Maudra.

Old Manddy's Song

Up and down the silver hall
Sweep, sweep, sweep
Tap of the broom in the quiet hall
Sweep, sweep, sweep

Morning sun through the windowpanes
Rise, rise, rise
Different yes but ever the same
Rise, rise, rise

Up and down the silver hall
Sweep, sweep, sweep
Tap of the broom in the quiet hall
Sweep, sweep, sweep

In the courtyard, watching the childlings play
Oh, oh, oh
Lassywings flying the day away
Oh, oh, oh

Up and down the silver hall
Sweep, sweep, sweep
Tap of the broom in the quiet hall
Sweep, sweep, sweep

Voices of children pretending to sleep
Now, now, now
Hush now the babes in the nursery
Now, now, now

Kira-Staba the Waystar and the Founding of Ha'rar

On a bluff overlooking Ha'rar, there is a grove of trees that glow bright and blue at night. Although one cannot see them from within Ha'rar itself—their light is blocked by the cliffs—a Sifan sailor told me that the light of the trees is visible from almost anywhere along the Silver Sea coast. She went on to say it is likely the reason Ha'rar was built here, as the early Vapra were enchanted by the light of the grove and, like Unamoths, followed the twinkling, thinking it was a guiding star. When they found it was, in fact, a grove of luminescent trees, they knew they had reached the place where they would build their legacy, and thus named the trees the Waystar Grove.

I visited the grove myself, with the help of a Vapran guide. It was not an easy journey. There were no paths carved into the sheer cliffs, and the wind off the sea rushing up the cliffs froze the tip of my nose, though my guide seemed impervious to the weather. When we reached the grove, it was near evening, and the lights from within the crystalline trees were just beginning to glow. I realized then that the grove is actually a single entity, growing in a ring like toadstools.

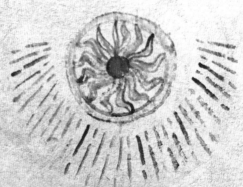

As the glow intensified, I felt as though the cold were nothing against my cheek. Watching the ring of trees slowly come to life is one of the most magical things I have ever seen. I can only imagine what it must have been like to be the early Vapran travelers, finally arriving at such a place. Whether or not the sailor's story of the Waystar's role in the founding of Ha'rar is true, it is certainly believable—decide for yourself.

The Forty Sisters

Many trine and many trine before
Forty sisters came
Pressed their hands on silver door
Opened wide to silver shore

Since many trine and many trine before
Forty sisters left
The nest that cradled them no more
And thrust them on the silver shore

For fifteen trine through lands unknown
Forty sisters wander
Along the silver beach alone
To find their eternal home

Then sixteen trine's horizon dawns
Finds forty sisters weary
But light upon the line is drawn
E'en after suns are set and gone

White like snow under full moons three
Forty sisters hopeful
Chased the light on the horizon seen
As if in an unending dream

Then to the mouth and cliffs and sea
Forty sisters fell
With tears of joy to eighty knees
At the foot of luminous Waystar trees

"Ha'rar, this place shall be named so,"
Forty sisters heard
From the star-like constellation grove
Crowned and cloaked in silver snow

And so Ha'rar, the silver mountain nest
Forty sisters built
And nestled within its snowy breast
Finally they lay themselves to rest

The Library

Though dozens of important buildings make Ha'rar a desired destination, it is perhaps the Vapran library that I found myself most in love with. This peaceful, domed building rests a few minutes' walk from the Citadel, built of white marble that matches the snow that dusts its thatched roof. Within, light shines through the stained glass in the ceiling's skylights, illuminating hundreds of thousands of tomes and scrolls. These precious—nay, sacred— artifacts are kept safe in the library, preserved and organized by fastidious librarians. These keepers of the books are also available to read aloud to others, as most Gelfling do not possess the skill of literacy. Like spell crafters or Sifan far-dreamers, they share the mysteries hidden in the countless writings with others, so that anyone may experience the magic within.

While perusing the books and breathing in the musty scent of their parchment, I became overwhelmed by the sheer volume of wisdom and song contained within a single building. So much lore could never be read by a single Gelfling during one lifetime. And yet, time seemed to slow while I wandered the stacks, peeking under pages and blowing dust from covers. Before I knew it, the lights from overhead were dark. I had been among the tomes all day, and yet my mind still ached with thirst for their ancient wisdom.

I thought it appropriate to include at least one song that I found in the archives of the library; I found it even more appropriate to select one about the library itself. This ode of delight is credited to a song teller who was present on the day the library building was completed, many, many trine ago.

Immortal House

Rest me in this immortal house
My head upon one thousand tomes
Lost within one thousand pages
Kept within a single room

Oh, ignites me more, does nothing else!
Than this place of paper, board, and string
The world without cannot compare
Nor make my song teller's lyre sing

This scent of etcher's burning palm
These inkèd sheets, these binded spines
Keep me captive and enchanted
In towers infinite and divine

For I would leave my life complete
Should I live until my final day
Resting within this immortal house
Bound forever by words that stay

A Final Word

On my last day among the Vapra, I said my goodbyes to my host family and took my time heading down the mainways of Ha'rar. I stopped to regard the library and the mountain bluffs visible at its back, promising this would not be the last time I stepped within those curved hallways lined with the words and songs of the Gelfling. That silver city, which I had always thought of as a mountain of frigid, unloving ice, had warmed to me. I had learned to see the rainbows that awaken when the sun shines through the coldest ice, learned to wait for the Unamoth that will someday emerge from the chrysalis. When bathing in the flames of the Gelfling fire, even the aloof Vapra become as the rest of us: Thoughtful. Caring. Gelfling.

The Grottan Clan

Grottan Mountains

Hidden away in the rocky Grottan Mountains, a network of clear freshwater rivers stream through indigo and black caves. Over thousands of trine, these rivers have carved tunnels and corridors, all of which convene in a beautiful underground lake. And here is where the Grottan Gelfling live—in a cavern hall called Domrak, buried within the Caves of Grot.

Although every Gelfling learns of this reclusive clan, the name of the Grottan is often the most any Gelfling ever know of them. Traveling to Domrak is a feat in itself, requiring not only an understanding of the maze of caves and tunnels, but also the ability to see in the dark in order to traverse them. And yet I can say with great confidence that despite the challenges in reaching Domrak and the Grottan clan, the journey was one of the most rewarding of all I have undertaken.

Though the Grottan are perceived by many outsiders as eerie and unnerving, these misconceptions are, at least in my experience, unfounded and based on fear of the unknown. And among the Gelfling clans, it could be argued the Grottan and their ways are the most unknown. Many things seem mysterious and frightening when they are done out of sight, in the shadows that most Gelfling fear. But the Grottan have learned to survive—and flourish—in these hidden places. And for that, I can find no other emotion in my breast except admiration. Though they may not see the suns of the "daylighter" world, they burn with a fire from within. And I learned from the Grottan that, unlike the fragile flames burning in torches and hearths, the light of the heart never goes out.

DAILY LIFE

The Grottan live quiet lives; not the
literal quiet of the often-silent Dousan,
but their activities are often independent
and rather focused. They are a small clan,
and close-knit. Childlings are schooled as
a group, where they learn basic alchemy
and other skills. As they grow older, they
are encouraged to apprentice and build
more specialized skills, in the hopes of
taking on the work one day themselves.
Meanwhile, the adults perform their
assigned tasks and duties, as given to
them by the maudra and her council
of elders.

The caves often seemed empty until one looked or listened more closely; then, in the still-seeming peace, one might see a Gelfling tending a fungus garden or measuring the levels of water down in the lake. Things are done at a slow but steady pace; Grottan tradition values the quality of a job well done over speed. Many Grottan daily activities require long periods of concentration and focus, which suits the quiet way in which many perform their work.

Worth mentioning as well is the Grottan observance of devotion to Thra and the Crystal of Truth. So deep within the earth and mountains, the caves are riddled with white Crystal veins pulsing with life force. Living in such an iridescent and sacred place, the Grottan have developed a profound and powerful love of the Crystal and Thra. Though the Gelfling mind is too small to dreamfast with the Crystal itself, the Grottan will often touch the Crystal ribbons and say quiet prayers, always with a loving and reverent expression. In this humble song teller's opinion, it would behoove any Gelfling to learn from the Grottan and practice such devotion to the Crystal that gives us our very life.

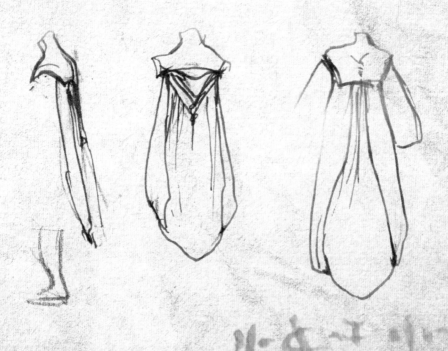

FINGER-TALK

The land of Domrak, though radiating from a central cavern, spans quite a distance if one were to measure the lengths of the corridors, tunnels, and connected caves. But unlike in a meadow or woodland, the various locations are separated by thick, impenetrable rock. A Gelfling voice—along with every other sound—bounces and echoes, becoming unintelligible by the time it reaches a Gelfling ear, and so calling to one another is impractical within the cave.

Thus, the Grottan have built a remarkable system for communication without the use of voice. It is called finger-talk, a descriptive name indeed, for it involves the tapping of fingers on cave walls in a specific pattern and rhythm. Similar to but far more sophisticated than the signal drums used by the Drenchen to communicate with rangers who have scouted into the swamp, Grottan finger-talk is as complete a language as our spoken word, able to relay complex meaning, location, and emotion. These signals can then be heard when one presses one's ear against the hard rock walls of the caves. Should you listen from anywhere within Domrak, you will hear a dozen or more conversations happening at any given time.

I tried to learn finger-talk while living with the Grottan, but I must admit I was very poor at it. This was frustrating for me, as a song teller. I am dexterous and, without much modesty, pride myself on being adept at learning foreign tongues (I speak Podling fluently and have even learned some Skeksis). Yet for whatever reason, in the beginning, finger-talk escaped me; I was only able, after many days' practice, to learn to signal my name—a convention used by Grottan to distinguish the "speaker" of a message among the many others communicated at the same time.

DAYLIGHTING

Grottan youth often whisper of daylighting—that is, the forbidden act of leaving the caves and venturing into the dangerous "daylighter" world and its excruciating brightness. The Grottan have built their lives within the caves, with a tradition that warns of the dangers beyond. Grottan eyes have developed such an aptitude for the dark that they are pained by any light more than the meager rays that pierce the rock ceiling above Domrak. While most Gelfling are blinded by the intense shadows of the caves, the Grottan are rendered the same when approaching the daylighter world—even on days that a Gelfling such as myself might find overcast and gloomy.

Daylighting is allowed by some; the maudra assigns the task to one or two Gelfling among the clan, who are seasoned at leaving the dark and traveling in the light. These daylighters make planned, highly organized trips to obtain ingredients and materials that cannot be found within the caves. And even though they embark on these trips with great confidence, they never make contact with other Gelfling if they can help it—not even the Stonewood, who neighbor in the forest to the southwest. Except for those who have been assigned to it by the maudra, daylighting is forbidden.

But of course, youngling curiosity is the same in Gelfling no matter the clan. I don't think I've met a single Grottan who didn't confess that at least once, as a youth, they snuck out of the comforting caves near Domrak, climbing upward toward the pinpricks of light. Their daylighting adventures vary, with some immediately blinded by the sun and unable to go farther than the cave exit, while others wrapped their faces in blindfolds or went during the night, tasting open air for the first time. From those who wandered into the wood a bit come tales of the thousand sounds of the forest and the howling of the wind; the rugged strength of the wind is a thing many comment on, having felt only hollow drafts in the caves before.

But no matter the adventures had, those who daylight always return most impressed by the same thing: the sky. Regardless of what time they left the caves or what else happened to them in their adventures, the sky was the most magnificent and terrifying thing they encountered. The sky, which the rest of us take for granted—big and open and vast, a window into space. Changing as a painter's canvas, depending on its unfathomable mood. The sky enchants the Grottan like nothing else, so much so that many dream of it for trine after their daylighting excursion.

Moontide

Like all bodies of water, the lake at the base of the Domrak cavern moves in tune with the Sister Moons. These tides may not generate waves as they do on the Silver Sea, but the rise and fall of the water levels does affect the Grottan's way of life. Using the waxing and waning of the lake, the Grottan are able to tell the passing of the seasons beyond the mountain caves.

When the lake rises to its highest point, the Grottan perform a ritual called Moontide. During this ritual, the Grottan maudra climbs to the bottom of the Domrak cavern and marks in the rock where the lake's waters touch the highest, labeling it with the number of the trine. In this way, the Grottan track the levels of the lake and the changing of the seasons.

I found this tracking of time to be an interesting paradox. The climate of the seasons has hardly any impact on life within the caves, except for the levels of water, which is only used as a measure of time. In every other aspect, the seasons have little meaning within Domrak. Indeed, the Grottan themselves take some pride in existing beyond the calendar of the daylighter world, set apart from the passing of time and the political seasons of the other clans. So why watch the water at all? Why track the passing of time? When I asked these questions of the elders, they told me politely to keep my nose in my own book.

THE MORNING SONG

So far removed from other Gelfling and the outside world, the caves of Domrak could sometimes drive me mad with their silence. Especially in the deep parts of the night, the only sound was the dripping of distant cave water, and sometimes the scurrying of some thirty-legged insect through the cracks in the walls above my bed. I wondered, in my first nights, how I would even know that the suns had risen in the world above. Without seeing their light, how would I know time was passing, when it was day and when it was night? How did the Grottan go about their lives without the sign of time passing readily visible in the sky?

This was my bias and misunderstanding, having been born and raised in the daylighter world. Of course, light did reach the caves, in small beams through tiny holes at the top of the Domrak ceiling. But small as they were, these spots of golden light traveled across the walls of the cavern, passing by carved marks. The marks and the sun spots indicated the time of day; the levels of the water in the lake showed the night passing.

And most lovely of all, every morning in Domrak begins with a single note from a Firca—joined shortly by a bow across strings, and then finally a voice. This chord, unbroken by the other sounds that plague the outside world, served as a replacement for the suns rising in the morning: gentle at first, warm, like dawn—growing until every rock within Domrak seemed to glow with awakening light.

SALVES AND ALCHEMY

The Caves of Grot provide a unique environment unlike any other inhabited by Gelfling. The lack of light and the consistent, cool temperatures make it an ideal place for storing ingredients that might otherwise spoil or become unstable. Thanks to this, many substances—from medicines to explosives—can be studied and manipulated without the risk of destroying them (or igniting them, as the case may be).

Grottan alchemists are among some of the most magically wise Gelfling I have ever met, able to mix moss and stone into a paste that heals wounds three times faster than the usual healing speed—and craft tiny packets of powder that ignite when set on fire. The applications of such powder spells range from clearing debris from collapsed tunnels to much smaller amounts used to frighten nesting Hollerbats from taking up roost in ventilation chutes.

There is a large overlap between Grottan alchemists and herbal sages. In fact, most I met were adept at both alchemy and medicine. When not bespelling minerals from one form into another, these wise elders do the same with organic materials. A favorite among Grottan are the spores and flesh of the thousands of fungus varieties common to the caves. Mushrooms, especially, thrive in the lightless caves, some emitting their own light with which they attract the insects that carry their spores throughout the caverns. There is even a type of glowing fungus that, once ingested, transfers its glowing properties to those who eat it! Grottan alchemists have endless knowledge of the different uses of fungi, from medicinal uses to poisons to the sliver of intersection between, using small amounts of toxic materials to heal illnesses stemming from the toxins of other creatures.

Hollerbats, Nurlocs, and Other Cave Creatures

The caves are home to many creatures, of which the Grottan consider themselves shepherds. Many are responsible for the daily task of bringing food to the creatures that cohabit in their dark space. The Nurlocs and the Hollerbats in particular have grown very accustomed to their daily and nightly feeding routines. The shepherds have learned over generations how to provide for the creatures, passing the wisdom of quantity and menu t hrough carefully preserved oral instructions.

In exchange, the Grottan benefit from the creatures in many ways; the Nurlocs loosen soil and rock as they dig, bringing aerated dirt into the caves as well as making conduits for fresh air. Without them, it would likely be impossible for Gelfling to survive within the caves. They also shed skin, fur, and scales, which are valuable materials for Grottan crafting; these durable remains are used in clothing, ornamenting, and the creation of instruments. The reedy antlers of the water variety of Nurloc, which fall off every thirty-four days, are hollow and make for very fine flutes.

Hollerbats—the Grottan's sigil creature—flock in enormous colonies within the caves. Although the Grottan sometimes complain about their constant and noisy companions, the truth is that life within Domrak would be cold and dark if it were not for the Hollerbats.

Upon studying these cave creatures, I've found that their dung is extremely flammable and, contrary to what you might believe, does not have a terrible smell when used in fire and torch burning. I was shocked at first to see the Grottan collecting the dung in barrels; Hollerbats cluster in colonies numbering in the thousands, and their droppings transform the floor of the caves they roost in. The stalagmites and mounds of the dung are collected when semi-fresh—just soft enough to break into manageable portions for transport. The dung is then combined with sterilizing and stabilizing salts by the Grottan apothecaries and made into a thick, viscous paste, which can be stored indefinitely in jars. The paste is applied to torch ends, lantern wicks, and the inner stones of hearths—anywhere one might want to see a long-lasting, cool-burning flame. Candles will burn for days if their tallow is mixed with the paste. For this reason, the paste is called everburn, an invaluable resource in the depths of Domrak.

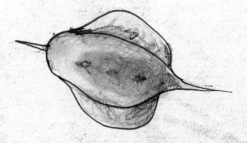

LIVING IN THE SHADOW OF THE ARATHIM

The caves that make up Domrak and its surrounding area were not all dug by the Grottan. In fact, some elders say most of the caverns are the remains of what was once an enormous Arathim nest—perhaps the original hive in which the ancient race spawned. However, the Arathim left the caves long ago, when the Skeksis arrived and gave Domrak to the Grottan, who have lived there ever since.

Before living among the Grottan, I did not know about the caves' previous inhabitants. When I first heard this rumor—that the cave in which I would rest my head every night was once a burrow of ten thousand Threaders—I thought that surely I was being told a joke. But as I read my diary within my cozy cave by the light of a candle, I looked closer. I saw the strange holes pocking the walls, just big enough to put my finger through. Hundreds of holes, dug by tiny Threaders, generations before the Grottan or I had arrived.

Signs like these were everywhere throughout the caves, once I knew to look for them, though many traces of the Arathim have been erased by the Grottan. Though, of course, all remains of webbing and silk have long since been removed, the Arathim are known for their "thread hooks"—the sculpting of stone on which to hang their webs. These hooks are large and conspicuous, but within Domrak, they have been crafted into other features by clever stonework and carving. Many of the bridges that span across the cavern are anchored on the thread hooks, to the point that they seem as if they could have been of Gelfling design instead of Arathim.

I asked if the Grottan ever thought the Arathim might return. They are known to roam aboveground, especially in the densest regions of the Endless Forest and among the highlands where Gelfling rarely go. The elders regarded my question as if I were a youngling, and as if every youngling asked the question at least once; their answer was that the Arathim would never return. Thra deigned to give the caves to the Grottan. If this were not so, why would Thra have evicted the Arathim to begin with?

The question—and its answer—became more abstract and philosophical from there, but my mind remained on the Arathim. The Arathim Ascendancy—the Threaders, Stingers, Spitters, and every other kind. Intelligent and loyal and powerful. Why would Thra have sent the Arathim away from this place to which they are so perfectly adapted only to be replaced by Gelfling, who commonly fear the dark rather than embrace it?

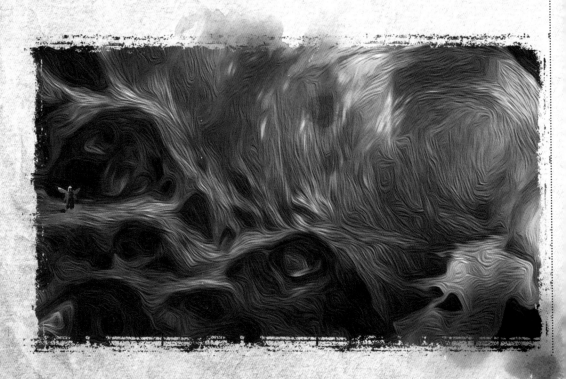

FOOD

The Caves of Grot reach straight into the heart of Thra, and it is no surprise that they are filled with flora, fauna, and fungi of a thousand varieties. Although they rarely seek game or ingredients from aboveground, the Grottan enjoy a wide array of foods. However, their rich menu of dishes was not the most delectable thing about their traditional cuisine; in fact, the way in which each meal was prepared was just as unique, thanks to their mind-boggling collection of spices and flavor dusts. Using everything from dried moss to salt-rock shaved from the interior walls of the caves, every Gelfling I met in Domrak had their own way of preparing even the most common of meals.

The Grottan diet consists largely of vegetarian fare, with large portions of mushrooms and root vegetables that are grown in cultivated colonies by Grottan farmers. Meals are often accented with a small amount of fish or seasoned paste. I was even lucky enough to try my first taste of dwarf Armalig, though to my understanding, such game is getting harder and harder to come by. The flavor reminded me of roast Nebrie. Leafy vegetables are a rare treat, as they only grow where sunlight reaches. When such things are included in a meal, the Grottan call it "dayfare," a phrase usually said with a half wink and a grumbling, hungry stomach.

Fascinating, too, were the Grottan's application of alchemy to food. They have developed ways of preserving foods by soaking them in vinegar, salt, and sugar. In this way they are able to store the rarer ingredients they find or procure from the daylighter world, and in addition, these pickling solutions lend very unique flavors to what might otherwise be a bland or boring ingredient.

Songs of the Grottan

The Myth of Aughra

Despite their disinterest in communing with their fellow Gelfling, the Grottan elders often invoked the name of Mother Aughra. Mother Aughra, the Helix-Horned; the three-eyed witch; the voice of Thra, if the old songs are to be believed. Of course, many songs tell of Aughra and her history of caring for us Gelfling; common tradition is to believe she brought us fire and water, earth and air; taught us to sing and dance; and explained to us the meaning of life and death.

If this is so, it has been hundreds of trine since those times, yet the Grottan speak of Aughra as if she were their friendly neighbor, living in a hut within the Grottan Mountains somewhere. Maudra Ermet told me that she often sends Nep, her young apprentice, out to the world beyond the caves to seek counsel from Aughra, or to trade with her Podling assistant for stocks of herbs and salves that are difficult to procure within the caves. In all my travels, I myself have not once seen a sign of Aughra—whether she is truly divine or just some old crone—so if this connection was contrived to impress me, I do not know.

The following is a wayfinding song, said to help a Grottan find their way to Aughra's famed orrery. Though, when I followed the steps detailed in the song, they took me wandering through the mountain woods until I became almost too lost to find my way back. I never saw the high hill with the promontory shaped like a cloud; I never reached the red vines. Regardless of my lack of success, I found it an insightful song and have recorded it herein.

The Way to the Observatory

Exit ye the Tomb of Relics
Climb the twelfth stair
Until you hear the sound of
Daylighter blowing air

Wait till nightfall if you must
Then leave the caves behind
Round the mossy waterfall
Down toward the falls ye climb

For all of night ye walk beside
The largest river stream
Then as the sky begins to light
A promontory ye will see

Upon a highest hill, belike
A cloud head of a storm
Head yonder and if ye lose sight
Let the suns your left cheek warm

With high hill as your marker
Journey make in two days' time
And when the river ends in rock
Up the rocky cliffside climb

A trail ye reach some distance up
Where red vines like long fingers grow
Whisper careful, boojay boojay
And into hidden tunnel go

Seven Tasks

Those who read deeply may have heard the legend of the Six Sisters, who were entrusted by Thra and the Crystal of Truth to found the seven clans and lead the Gelfling. Thra also assigned each of the sisters a nature and a divine task. The sisters went forth, and from their footsteps and hands sprang the Gelfling as flowers from the soil.

Though this origin myth, taking place long before even the Skeksis appeared in our world, is not regarded by most Gelfling as the true beginnings of our seven clans, the Grottan in particular are quite loyal to it. Perhaps this is because the song was told—if rumors are to be believed—by a Grottan. The legend of this song's inspiration is a song in itself, and the framing for the song of the Six Sisters:

Song of the Six Sisters

Hidden within the ancient Tomb
Sylus, Grottan song teller, lay
   sleeping
When dream he had, his hand
   outspread
The makings of an etching

When he woke, he saw the mark
Proof of his magic far-dreaming
So he looked upon it and softly
   read
What he'd sung while he'd been
   resting:

A thousand trine and more ago
The land was calm before
No Gelfling walked below the
   trees
Nor sailed the windy shore

Then rise up from the flower bed
Sweet Gelfling, sisters six
And the Crystal turned its song
   to them
Within their dreams transfixed

"Awaken, hear my dreaming song
Ye Sisters, two times three
So seven clans may spring forth
I entrust these seven gifts to ye:

To the Dousan, the endless heavens;
   the study of the skies
To the Sifa, the changing wind;
   the telling of signs
To the Stonewood, the burning fire;
   the essence of the hearth
To the Spriton, the protective
   land; the foundation of the
   earth
To the Drenchen, the vital water;
   the blue flame of life
To the Silver Sea clan, the records
   of shadow and light."

Six sisters woke from their dream
And tearfully parted ways
Into six clans their gardens grew
For a hundred nights and days

But Thra's voice had spoken seven
So the great clan of the Silver Sea
Split in twain and separated
To fulfill Thra's fated prophecy:

The sixth became the sixth and
   seventh
Cursed and blessed, dark and
   bright
The Grottan and the Vapra
One in shadow, one in light

So read the dream-etched book
   of Sylus
As he looked upon the dreamed
   tome
He closed the cover and left it
   hidden
Where it belonged within the Tomb

111

The Tomb of Relics

Perhaps one of the most sacred locations maintained by the Grottan Gelfling is the Tomb of Relics, a catacomb of halls some half day's distance from Domrak. Within the halls, protected by a heavy stone door, is an unending collection of artifacts gathered from throughout history. Tapestries, tools, artwork, and even books line shelves and fill crates, making up potentially the most comprehensive assortment of Gelfling treasures in existence.

One question I asked, of course, was who is responsible for finding such items and bringing them here. To this the Grottan had varying answers, ranging from Gelfling adventurers to Aughra herself. One youth even suggested that she had once seen a pale four-armed creature moving about the Tomb, mumbling to itself. These songs of fancy imbue the Tomb with a most mysterious charm.

There is a game played by the Grottan called Gricksies, which is based loosely on the layout of the Tomb. The following is a short ditty about the game and the Tomb, usually sung by parents while tending to their infants.

Gricksies

Over, under, over, under
Weave through Gricksies maze
Forward, backward, round the corner
Right and left and sideways

Toss the stones and shells and gems
Before the candle burns out
Clicky clacky running backsies
Gricksies! Everyone has struck out

The Sanctuary

The Sanctuary, a grand valley in the heart of the mountains, is one of the few locations the Grottan frequent that is outside the caves. Judging from the petrified aquatic plant formations—including giant lily pads and fungi—as well as the shallow water at the very base of the gorge, I believe the open valley may have once been a mountaintop lake, perhaps even the elusive headwaters of the famous Black River.

Here in the Sanctuary—only at night, when the light of the suns does not bother their sensitive eyes—the Grottan Gelfling meditate upon the Song of Thra, which they say can be heard here better than anywhere else in the Skarith Land. Whether this is true or not, I have no authority to say. All I can add is that, with the wide sky above and the deep earth opening into the belly of the world below, I have never felt so much an intermediary between the Crystal of Truth and the rest of Thra as I did within the Sanctuary.

This Grottan chant bears a resemblance to other meditative chants I have heard among Gelfling of other clans. I am told it invokes the four elements in the language of Thra:

Grottan Meditation Chant

Arugaru aru agura aru
Deatea dea deratea tea
Kidakida ki kira kida

Every seven hundred trine, song tellers say, Bell-Birds roost in the Sanctuary. Though I did not see any of these magnificent creatures during my stay, I came across evidence of their passing in the form of enormous stone nests and loose feathers longer than I am tall. It reminded me of one of Gyr the Song Teller's most famous love ballads, which I include herein.

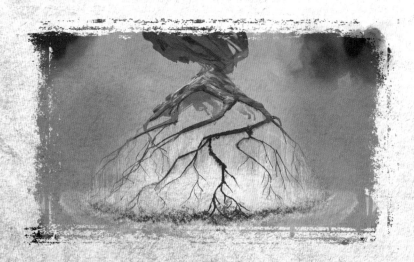

The Bell-Bird and the Mountain
(Attributed to Gyr the Song Teller)

Let me tell you a song of these windy peaks
Whose stories fill hearts like a fountain
This song of a love ne'er meant to be
The Bell-Bird and the Mountain

As you know, every seventh ninet spring
The Bell-Birds flock to the Sanct of Grot
Where they roost, line their nests, warble and sing
Echoing songs of the past that the rest have forgot

One Bell-Bird arrived long after the others
No mate would she find left around them
But sad she was not of the burgeoning mothers
For her love was the very mountain

It had echoed her call since the beginning of time
No matter where she called from, it responded
Through perfect refrain in a mirroring rhyme
The Bell-Bird and mountain were bonded

For hundreds of trine, the Bell-Bird returned
Ne'er roosted, nor nested, nor a single egg laid
But happy she was with the light that she burned
And never once from her sweet mountain strayed

Through trine and unum, wind, storm, and snow
The Bell-Bird grew old on her love's cliffside face
Though to her soft murmurs it never first spoke
She died happily there in its stony embrace

Vliste-Staba, the Sanctuary Tree

Above the caves, flourishing in the thin mountain air, is Vliste-Staba, the Sanctuary Tree. This magnificent, pink-petaled tree is visible from many peaks in the Grottan range; its bright hue is impossible to miss, especially as it flowers three seasons out of the trine, only shedding its blossoms in late winter. The Sanctuary Tree is also called "the mirror of the mountains," perhaps alluding to one of the Grottan's more romantic songs, which I have scribed here.

Because of the reference in the song, some Grottan elders believe that the Sanctuary Tree has two faces: *As if looking at itself in the reflection of a mountain lake*, they told me. Does this mean the Sanctuary Tree has a twin, hidden somewhere in the caves? Were I a Grottan myself and able to see in the dark, I might risk a journey even farther into the belly of the mountains . . . but alas, I am unequipped for such an adventure, as much as it pains me. And so, all I have as evidence of this mysterious reflection of the Sanctuary Tree is this song:

The Mirror of the Mountain

Gaze she now upon her feet
Pink petals dance on surface
Stone pebbles sink in water deep
Through the mirror of the mountain

A Final Word

When my time with the Grottan came to an end, I left at dusk with a pouch of glowing moss and a collection of traveler's salves. Returning to the daylighters' world after living in Domrak was like being born into a new world; I felt as if I were seeing it for the first time. As I waited in the shade for the burning in my eyes to subside, I pressed my ear against a stone and could hear the tapped words of the Grottan sending their farewells. Though still clumsy in spite of my practice, I touched the rocks and told them of my gratitude as best I could. Then I listened to the stones as I had when I was a childling in Stone-in-the-Wood, though this time, accompanied by the chorus of my Grottan friends, I felt as though I could hear more of the Song of Thra than ever before.

THE
SIFA CLAN

Cera-Na

The Silver Sea borders the northern shore of our world, vast and cold, especially in the winters, when the ice shelves grow along the coast in frigid, crystalline formations. Yet even in the coldest of seasons, should one look out into the frothing waves, it won't be long before a spark of color pricks through the flurries of snow. Red and purple and indigo sails and banners, warm and bright as the fires of prophecy: Sifan ships, sailing in small convoys of three or four, in transit between their home port of Cera-Na and their innumerable adventures at sea.

The Sifa's routes thread west from the northern Silver Sea, then loop down to the south along the windward side of the Claw Mountains. Their ships are particularly adapted to traverse these difficult waters, and therefore many have called this westerly band of rough water the Sifa Coast. To the Sifa, it is Sa-Schala, the Mariner's Paradise.

Of course, one cannot discuss the Mariner's Paradise without mentioning Cera-Na. This coastal village, made up of an eternally changing population of sailors coming in and out of port, is nestled in a bay on the ocean side of the Claw Mountains. The bay is protected from the harsh ocean winds by the cliffs, its waters calmer than those of the open ocean and a safe haven for ships that may have taken recent damage during their dangerous voyages at sea. Although Cera-Na enjoys some trade with the Dousan, who neighbor on the other side of the mountains, its visitors are primarily Sifa.

However, for those
traveling to and from Ha'rar
along the scenic trails that
shoulder the coast, ever-lit
wayfarer's lanterns mark the
way every hundred paces. The
firelight in these Hooyim-shaped
lanterns flickers eternally, visible
even through the dense silver fog
that cloaks the shore from twilight
until dawn.

DAILY LIFE

Life on the sea is dictated by the whims of the elements and the skill of the sailors who traverse it. Calm days become stormy with hardly any warning—or one moment you may be staring down a hurricane and fearing for your life, and the next you're gazing at the most beautiful, clear sky without a care or worry. Food and water appear and vanish like mirages, in shoals of fast-moving fish or early morning rain—if one does not know where to look, one might quickly miss any of the million things happening at any given time.

And so the Sifan way of life is to live in the moment. To value what is happening when it is happening, and to never rely too much on what one has—for at any moment, it could be gone. The most important things, living this way, are what brings joy, what one can remember of one's past despite what might have been swept away, and what makes each Sifa who they are.

Although the currents that carry their ships are often unpredictable, thousands of trine at sea have endowed the Sifa with a knowledge of signs that, to an outsider such as myself, can seem prophetic. Reading the shapes of clouds and the pointed peaks of the waves, a skilled Sifan sailor can see a storm coming days in advance. It is this same skilled, specialized perception that may have evolved into the prophetic abilities of far-dreamers, who are able to read the otherwise imperceptible signs within a Gelfling heart. Indeed, reading signs and obeying them is perhaps one of the most important aspects of Sifan tradition—so much so that ignoring a sign can be considered offense enough to be left behind on a forsaken shore.

SAMAUDREN

The Sifa, unlike many of the other Gelfling clans, do not sail, or live for that matter, in a single large group. Though they congregate at Cera-Na for important occasions, most Sifa travel in small groups of Gelfling, usually numbering six ships or fewer. These intimate groups, called samaudren ("sea brethren"), operate as a single unit. They sail together, sleep together, fish together, and eat together. When bringing their catch to market, they work together as well, sharing in whatever bounty they secure as trade.

During my time with the Sifa, I was welcomed by a samaudren of four ships, considered lucky. As a song teller, my daily work was straightforward and—I often felt—overvalued; thanks to the long distances between destinations, a song is often considered a luxurious commodity. I was glad for this, since I have very few other talents to provide in exchange for the friendly, almost familial, kindness and generosity that I experienced with my host samaudren.

Another aspect of samaudren, similar to Dousan xerics, is that the leader of these smaller groups is not always a woman. The leader of my samaudren was a spindly elder with a beard long gone white. But despite his gender and lack of wings, he was still able to leap between the masts and lines with the grace and agility of any maudra.

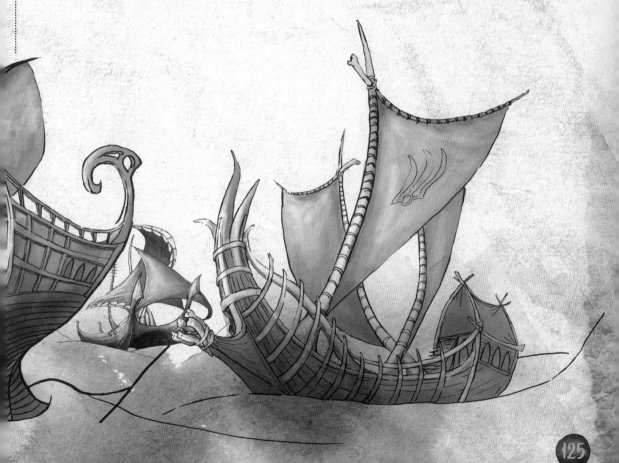

ERA-IANEM, THE WIND IN THE SAIL

One thing I loved most about the Sifan tradition of samaudren was the idea that family is not a bond of blood but one of directionality. This philosophy is called *era-ianem*, meaning "wind in the sail," and comes from a Sifan proverb, *Care not what fabric makes your sails, but what wind fills them.*

The idea of *era-ianem* is that, while we are all made of blood and flesh, what we do with our lives is of our own invention. This is a philosophy that is contrary to many other Gelfling traditions, which place blood relation and clan loyalty above all other bonds. I saw how *era-ianem* was applied among the samaudren; these small groups often included blood family, but just as often were made up of unrelated friends who had created their own family.

Shockingly, one samaudren I encountered had even extended their bonds of *era-ianem* to a Gelfling who had not been born Sifa. At first when I met this individual, I thought she was, like me, a traveler who had gone to sea with the Sifa to learn their ways. In fact, this was how it began, but after many trine sailing with the Sifa, she found that among their crimson sails was where her heart belonged. When she expressed her desire to join them, her samaudren welcomed her. They invoked *era-ianem* before the maudra of the clan, and she opened her arms to embrace this Vapra as one of her own. It was unlike anything I have ever seen before. Although I found it very peculiar, I wonder if one day such things might be an example of the Sifa's forward-thinking ways— and if such boundless inclusion might become more common over time.

FAR-DREAMERS

While they can be easy to spot, the Sifa can be difficult to catch. Even when they make port in Ha'rar for trade, they never stay for long. Though one might try to predict when the Sifa will arrive or depart based on the tides or the season, ultimately one will fail. The Sifa chart their courses based on thousands of signs interpreted by their renowned far-dreamers, who read the stars, waves, and everything in between. Though far-dreamers have been found among other clans, it seems that there is something special about the life of the Sifa Gelfling that cultivates the natural talents of the soothsayer. Whether it is the unfettered access to the stars, or perhaps thanks to a life constantly in motion, I cannot say.

Far-dreamers hear the Song of Thra in a way unlike other Gelfling. If the wind is the breath of the world, where most of us might feel it gently upon our cheek, a far-dreamer hears a thousand words within the same breeze, and sees a thousand visions more. When a far-dreamer speaks, Thra listens; when a far-dreamer sleeps, they settle deeply into the current of the world until they are fully enveloped.

Although the Sifa affiliate themselves with wind—for it fills their sails and determines their destinies—far-dreamers often incorporate the element of prophecy, fire, into their methods, whether through open flames in candles or torches, or items that have been burned—called *yabo*, "fire-touched." *Yabo* are frequently sticks of incense or bundles of dried herbs, though sometimes far-dreamers use metal medallions or other tougher substances that have been blessed by fire.

I saw several far-dreamers when I sailed with the Sifa, and my experiences varied. Sometimes I felt as though I was talking to an old friend, but often they did not even seem to be conscious of when I sat with them; the room was silent, filled only with the scent of Sifan herbs lingering in the air. During one such encounter, we sat in quiet for a long time, at the end of which the far-dreamer spoke only two words: "Say yes." To this day, I still do not know what it meant.

SKEKSA THE MARINER

Despite a life detached from the mainland, which revels in the glory of the Skeksis, the Sifa still maintain the utmost respect for the lords. Many Sifan ships have a carving or amulet of skekSa the Mariner fastened to the prow, as a way to ward off turbulent weather and seek luck.

When I asked the Sifa about skekSa, the answers varied. Some of the Sifa regarded the Skeksis Mariner with the same distance that other Gelfling—the Vapra of Ha'rar, for example—regard the other lords. That is to say, with respect, and acknowledging that it is impossible for a Gelfling to know a Skeksis, just as it is impossible for us to know the suns or the moons or the Crystal.

Yet others—the maudra included—spoke of skekSa in an unnervingly familiar way. As if their interactions went beyond that of Gelfling to Skeksis Lord; as if the Mariner were more of a patron guide than a superior being of transcendent wisdom and power. While it thrilled my song teller's senses to regard a Skeksis as a mortal creature that might deign to interact with the Gelfling in this way, it was also terrifying to imagine.

However the Sifa spoke of the Mariner, I was never able to witness their interaction with my own eyes directly. I saw evidence of the Skeksis Mariner only once, and then only from afar. As we approached Cera-Na after a long voyage, I sighted the maudra's coral ship on the horizon. Beside it was a mound as tall and large as an island, broken with spikes like mountains. It was Lord skekSa's ship, my Sifan guide explained. But before I could ask further, the great ship submerged, and I never saw it again.

HOOYIM BOAT RACES

One of the most exciting events that I had the pleasure of partaking in were the Hooyim boat races. The Sifa treasure the Hooyim, the multicolored, jewel-scaled fish that swim in schools of thousands near the coasts. When the weather becomes warmest, the glittering shoals ride the coastal waters toward Cera-Na—and so too do the Sifa.

There hundreds of Sifa gather with their windships, hulls painted and sails dyed to match the brilliant colors of the Hooyim. These small, one-Gelfling windships are built during the cooler seasons every trine, polished and balanced to perfection for the races, which take place in honor of their sigil creature.

In small pods of twelve, the sailors compete in races of speed and agility. The courses run along shallow waters, at first unbroken, but then into the places where the rocky landforms break the waves. Here the navigation becomes perilous, and only the most experienced and brave of the sailors endeavor to

pass through. Many skiffs break against the stony fingers, at the mercy of the unpredictable water eddies and gusts of wind. Injuries are common, and there is sometimes death; but this is the life these sailors live, I suppose.

When a winner finally reaches the finish goal—sometimes by being the only skiff remaining—they are anointed with a winner's dye: a spot of ink from the thumb of the maudra, placed upon their brow, which lasts for several days so all can see their mark of victory. In the evening, after the races are over, all the skiffs (or what remains of them) are brought to the beach and burned in an extravagant bonfire, complete with song and dance.

Sifan boat racing, more than almost any other tradition, seems to bring every Sifan value into one exciting, fast-paced event. To know one's ship is to know one's self; to navigate the dangerous course requires the most skilled observance of the signs of Thra. And, of course, to survive against the odds—and especially to emerge triumphant, marked and lauded by the entire clan—is perhaps the dream of any Gelfling, Sifa or not.

Sifan Charms

I was reluctant in the beginning to ask my Sifan hosts about their many enchanted amulets, talismans, and charms, but when one of my closer friends noticed my intrigued gaze, I actually found them to be surprisingly forthcoming about the significance of their many trinkets. One after the other, my Sifan friends told me the stories of their pretties and shinies.

To write of every one of the charms would require a scroll all its own. The charms are made of nearly every material known to Gelfling. Some are quite common, such as charms braided from old sailcloth or carved from splinters of ship wood from a decaying vessel. Shells, scales, and pieces of coral are also very popular, along with driftwood and other small items that are easy to find on the shore or within the shallows along the coasts. Rarer trinkets I saw included precious gems and metals, some in their raw state wrapped with wire, others carved or refined into beautiful amulets. Most of the charms are made of materials resistant to water and sea air, for obvious reasons, though some of the more fragile charms—feathers, for example—are kept in small glass vials.

One thing the charms do all have in common is that they were all collected as mementos. The Sifa wear colored cord (sometimes interwoven with chains of precious metals) to which the amulets are attached. The color of the cord signifies what the Sifa call directionality; red for the past, purple for the present, and blue for the future. The charms are attached to the different cords, indicating the direction in which the wearer wishes to take those memories. For example, charms that are mementos of positive events or beloved friends are often strung high on the blue cord. Sad memories are sometimes strung low on the red cord to be left in the past—though one of my hosts told me she prefers to bring her sad memories along the blue cord to remind her of the troubles she has overcome and the strength she has gained since.

DAY OF THE ROSE SUN

To the Sifa, the passing of the suns and moons is crucial to their maritime and spiritual schedule. The Day of the Rose Sun, in particular, appeals to the Sifa—perhaps because of its reddish hue, or because this day marks the change of the coastal winds that carry the Sifa to and from Cera-Na to Ha'rar. Once these winds and tides change, the Sifa migrate farther west, many not seen again until the winds return to their easterly routes.

To the Sifa, the Rose Sun represents fire and rebirth, as the winds shift. Many Sifa celebrate this change of season and direction in the traditional Gelfling way, with meditation and observance of the sun's path through making and lighting candles. This makes for a lovely image, especially among many Sifan ships in the evening, as if the stars themselves have come to rest along the

reflective silver waters and froth-capped waves. Some Sifa release the candles into the air in dyed paper lanterns, specially made to catch fire when they reach great heights, igniting in balls of multicolored flame overhead before dissolving into silvery ash.

Another Day of the Rose Sun tradition that seems exclusive to the Sifa is hair doll making. Especially popular among Gelfling adolescents, who are just beginning to experience the world as young adults, hair doll making is an activity wherein one cuts locks of one's hair and wraps them with cord in the form of a Gelfling. These hair dolls are meant to resemble their maker, a self-portrait, complete with clothing made from scraps of their maker's coats and capes. In the evening on the Day of the Rose Sun, while the candles flicker from every boat prow and rail, the dolls are tossed into the boat fires. In this way, the young Sifa open themselves to being born anew among the smoke and embers.

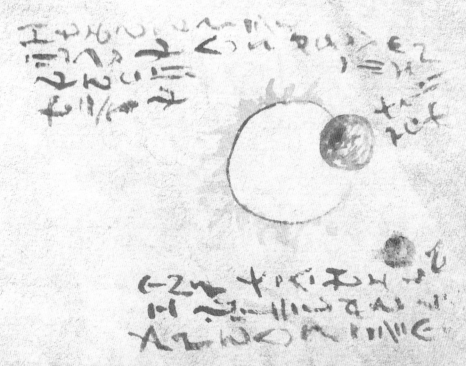

FOOD

It should be no surprise, of course, that the Sifan diet is comprised mainly of fish and sea creatures. Prior to my time traveling and living with them, I had always thought such fare to surely be tiresome. But since tasting the hundreds of aquatic delights served to me by my Sifan hosts, I have learned that the bounty of the sea is just as—if not more—varied as that of the land and wood. I have tasted urchin and shellfish, Hooyim and giant *usi*. Meatless kelp dishes seasoned with sea salt, and rockfish from the bottom of the ocean. I have even become proficient with a Sifan rod, and feel confident that, stranded on a ship alone, I would never starve, as long as I had a means to fish.

Although nearly everything on a Sifan platter comes from the sea, they do keep a stock of some mainland ingredients: spices that cannot be procured or approximated on the sea, grains, and some of the harder cheeses, which do not spoil. Most important, my Sifan hosts explained, were fruits and vegetables. Though some larger Sifan ships have room aboard for small herb gardens, it is impossible to keep a larger garden at sea. And so, the Sifa frequently trade their catches and finds at port, namely in Cera-Na and Ha'rar.

Sifan cuisine favors bold flavors, especially fire dust, a spice made from grinding flame coral, which can be found in the shallow waters along the western Sifa Coast. This hot flavor pairs deliciously with the more subtle flavors of deep-sea fish and shellfish.

Songs of the Sifa

Gyr the Song Teller

As a song teller myself, of course I am well versed in the ballads of Gyr, who sailed long ago. The Sifa take great pride in Gyr's work; although we cannot say for sure, most historians say Gyr was of the Sifa clan, and his wanderlust, compassionate heart, and gift of song are attributes highly praised by the Sifa. So, since his time, the Sifa have kept his songs alive.

Here is one of my favorites among Gyr's thousand songs, told to me by a spritely Sifan elder when we made port in Cera-Na for an evening, as we sat beside a blazing bonfire, the younglings throwing dust into the fire to make it spark, the night sky passing dark and blue above us.

The Wayfarer's Lanterns

Now I leave port for the Silver Sea
To be lost in the waves and the ocean breeze
But the wayfarer's lanterns will call to me
Yes, the wayfarer's lanterns, to me

In the night, when the land melts into the sky
And the embers above like the fireflies fly
Then the eyes of the stars call to me
Yes, the eyes of the stars, to me

In the day, when the ocean is all I can see
Flat and blue below a sky cloudless and free
The smiles of the Brothers shine on me
Yes, their smiles shine down on me

In the evening, when the Sisters quietly wake
And in their blue cloaks, their night walk make
Their sweet singing voices rain down on me
Yes, their songs rain down on me

Now long have I been on the Silver Sea
My journeys have made me so full and weary
And the wayfarer's lanterns, they call to me
Yes, the wayfarer's lanterns, to me

While the Sifa have preserved hundreds of Gyr's songs, both in mind and tongue as well as on paper and tablet, since his time, many songs have also been written and told about his legendary adventures. One of the most well-told songs about Gyr is one I actually heard among the Spriton, far from the Silver Sea. The fact that word of his adventures has traveled so far from the Sifa Coast certainly speaks to Gyr's widespread popularity among song tellers.

Sign of the Three Sisters

Gyr was a bard who traveled the seas
Oh li, oh la, oh lo
Told the songs of the rivers, the mountains, the trees
Oh li, oh la, la-lo

One long summer ago, the night stopped to come
The Sister Moons hiding, in fear of the suns
The daylight was endless, scorching the plains
So Gyr went to find them and bring night again
He found two of the moons at the edge of the sky
A lake at their feet from the tears they had cried
"The Brother Suns' fire for us is too bright
While they rage in the sky we cannot bring the night
So we Sisters take turns going first into dawn,
To spy on the Brothers to see if they've gone

'Twas our second Sister Moon's turn to go
Oh li, oh la, oh lo
But the second Brother Sun ate her whole
Oh li, oh la, la-lo

The moons were too fearful since their Sister's sad fate
To bring night to the sky, to bring nine to the eight
So Gyr left them to watch the Brother Suns from the land
He returned three days later and told them his plan
The remaining two Sisters scaled the edge of the sky
Their fingertips wet from the tears that they'd cried
From their lips came a song: a mournful, sad sigh
And from the belly of the sun came a lonely reply
For the second Sister was still alive
Oh, the second Sister was still alive

To this day, though she's hidden by Brother Sun's light
Oh li, oh la, oh lo
Her song tells her Sisters to bring out the night
Oh she, oh sha, she knows
To bring out the night
Oh she, oh sha, she knows

Beyond his legendary songs and the songs of his adventures, some tales even suggest that Gyr may have had extraordinary powers. Of course, the talents and abilities of many folk heroes are exaggerated. During my travels (not only with the Sifa), I heard many songs speaking of Gyr's surprising magical gifts, from the ability to speak in the Skeksis' native tongue to a far-dreaming-like ability to transcend space and time, granted to him after a stay on a strange uninhabited island in the middle of the untraveled sea.

So, when I had the chance to mingle with Sifan song tellers, I was eager to know their opinions. In spite of the extravagant claims I had heard elsewhere, the Sifan bards were terribly casual about their ancestor, agreeing that it was unlikely Gyr was the sorcerer of words many make him out to be. However, one ability that was more or less agreed upon was that Gyr was in possession of a sacred Firca that he dream-crafted himself from the bone of a Bell-Bird.

Bell-Birds, while scarce in our day, are one of the few remaining creatures able to speak to stone. One is particularly blessed if one hears the echoing, ground-shaking, mountain-shivering call of a Bell-Bird, ringing out across the Skarith Land and audible from halfway across the world. Thus, it is not surprising that the songs told about Gyr's mythical bone Firca say it was an instrument of incomparable power. One song in particular, written here, tells that the images and words of Gyr's heart were etched into stone when he played upon the flute.

Gyr and the Bone Firca

Took he in his hand, Gyr the Song Teller
A bone of the Bell-Bird fallen
And the Bell-Bird collar
Dreamed he with heated fingertips the shape
Of all the songs of the 'verse

Every sound that rises from any
Wailing childling or old mauddy
The blue lifeblood aglow
Like steam from the seas as they touch
The shore, this song of the heart

Ere, across the faces of every cavern
Etched as rhymes on a still heart
Hot as truth on a cold lie
Dream-fastened through the power
Of the Bell-Bird's song

The Mariner Star

The Sifa are loyal and passionate in their adoration of Lord skekSa the Mariner, leading them to name several constellations after their enigmatic idol. As the stars are often the only means of navigation on the sea, especially in the dark, when even nearby landforms are invisible, the Sifa have long used Lord skekSa's features to characterize the night sky: For example, the Behemoth, a low-lying constellation visible far to the south, is named Vassafina after skekSa's legendary beast of burden. And to the north is a bright configuration called the Mariner Star. Always visible, this constellation is actually three stars in close proximity. Some have illustrated it as Lord skekSa's tricorn hat; others have envisioned it as representing the Three Sisters in star form. In turn, the Three Sisters are often represented in Sifan illustrations thus: skekSa as the Blue Moon, the Sifa as the Pearl Moon, and a mysterious entity called San as the Hidden Moon.

Whatever the representation, the light of the Mariner Star is fundamental to Sifan sailing, providing an eternal indicator of true north. Thanks to its constant shining, the Sifa sing dozens of devoted songs to this star, often overlapping with their thanks to and adoration of their patron Skeksis. The following is a song usually told by old sailors when they make port at Cera-Na and are eager to return to the open sea.

Ode to the Mariner Star

Shine, shine, shine
We sail below, below
The Mariner Star aglow

Shine, shine, shine
Sun, moon, star
We sail afar, afar

Shine, shine, shine
Bathe us awhile
In our Lord Mariner's smile

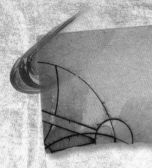

Omerya-Staba, the Coral Tree

During my time with the Sifa, I had the joy of visiting Cera-Na three times. On the third and final arrival, as we came around the rocky isthmuses that surround the port, I was stunned to see a great coral structure in the center of the bay. It blossomed up and out of the water like a flower. The throngs of smaller Sifan ships looked like minnows in comparison. As we drew closer, I realized that the ivory and carmine reef was a vessel—an enormous ship built within a moving reef, accented with sails and rigging and a deck.

I was told its name: Omerya-Staba, or the Coral Tree. The Sifan maudra's vessel. At her command, its sails unfurl and fill with wind, the rudders and fins built into the sides of the reef extend, and though it is thirty times the size of the other Sifan ships, it sails just as smoothly and easily.

Like the patron trees of the other Gelfling clans, the Omerya is regarded as the mother of the community. When it is in Cera-Na, there is always great jubilation; like a flock of birds, the Sifan ships congregate from all corners of the sea just to bask in the great Coral Tree's radiance. So lovely is the tree that even the close-lipped Dousan cannot help but marvel at the sight when they come to trade in Cera-Na. The following is a song I heard from a Dousan sandmaster's bard:

The Sifa Mother of Sa-Schala

Have you never seen such a drop of water upon a wave
As the Sifa Mother in the palm of Cera-Na?
Like a flower blooming
With her children blossoming
The Sifa Mother in the palm of Cera-Na

Have you never spied such a twinkling in the starlit sky
As the Omerya in the bay of the Silver Sea?
Like a torch a-burning
With her sails unyielding
The Omerya in the bay of the Silver Sea

Have you never felt such a cool shade on the warm sand
As the Sifa Mother of Sa-Schala?
Like a cool wind blowing
With her tendrils flowing
The lovely Sifa Mother of Sa-Schala

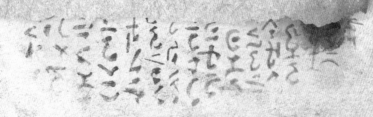

Thanks to my Sifan hosts, I was able to gain an audience with Maudra Affina aboard the Omerya. The deck of the ship is built of long planks that create an even surface on the top of the ship, and in the center of the vast deck is a stone hearth that is always alight with scented fire. Here the maudra's far-dreamers gather, spying in the smoke the signs that will guide the Omerya, and thus, the rest of the clan. For although the Sifa do not always flock together, they are loyal, and whatever course the maudra sets, the rest of the clan will embark upon it with every sail unfurled.

The masts of the ship are coral spires, reinforced with timber and heavy Sifan rope—only in this way are they able to contain the sails necessary to move such a large vessel. The maudra's crew is at least a hundred Gelfling strong, all of whom live their entire life aboard the Omerya serving the tree and its maudra captain. They taught me the following call-and-response song often sung by the Omerya's sailors while they prepare the ship for a voyage.

Oh My Omerya

Do you hear me, oh my Omerya?—I wake to the sound of your song
Believe in me, oh my Omerya—I have been sleeping on shore too long

Do you yearn for the sea, oh my Omerya?—I hunger for horizons unbroke
Protect me, oh my lovely Omerya—I have sheltered you since I awoke

Do your sails crave the wind, oh my Omerya?—Stretch them and see, my child
Dance with me, oh my Omerya—I will take us out into the wild

Does your hull thirst for saltwater, Omerya?—Yea, my reefing aches for the waves
Wait for me, oh my Omerya—Light the fires and hoist your staves

A Final Word

I felt a great swaying beneath my feet the day my Sifan friends brought me to shore in Cera-Na. I stepped off our tiny, sturdy ship and onto the dock, holding to the post as my feet yearned for the waves. As we said our tearful goodbyes, I was given my first and only Sifan charm: a braid made from strips of sailcloth from the four ships within our samaudren. When asked where I would travel next, I realized I did not know—but for the first time, that did not frighten me. I would go where the wind would take me.

The Dousan Clan

Claw Mountains

The Endless Forest may seem to sprawl forever in every direction, but even this wood has its boundaries. On the northwestern-most perimeter of the forest, the trees are anything but green and lush. Dry, salty dunes lap at their roots in rippling waves of shining crystal sand. Here, marked by a long line of dead trees bleached by the three suns, the Endless Forest ends and the great Crystal Desert begins.

It is not easy living on the sands of the Crystal Desert. Except for along the northern edge, where the Claw Mountains rise tall and red, there are very few structures to provide shade. Any moisture in the air that lands during the night evaporates almost immediately. But that doesn't mean the desert is devoid of life. Though all is still one moment, in the next a pod of

one hundred Crystal Skimmers bursts through the dunes, spraying crystal sand and sending rainbows flashing across the sky. These explosions of life and adventure characterize the desert, breaking the silence and stillness like lightning. One cannot remain still in such a place, nor can one become complacent.

The Dousan Gelfling are no different. Taking advantage of their long tradition of bone carpentry and their keen understanding of the desert's weather, these nomads go where the sands take them aboard their sand skiffs of bone, crafted from the found remains of desert creatures. Countless generations inform their complex traveling patterns, and although I would have been lost without them, when I was with them, I found life on the Crystal Desert to be as fruitful as any.

DAILY LIFE

Dousan daily life centers around communion with Thra and the Crystal, acknowledgment of the passing of time, the humility of mortality, and the divinity of the Crystal of Truth. Dousan rituals and prayers omit the Skeksis—a heresy only allowed because of the Dousan's remote location, far from the castle, to be sure—and acknowledge Mother Aughra not as a sacred child of the Crystal and the voice of Thra, but as any other mortal creature who walks the land as Gelfling do.

A day in the Crystal Desert consists of two categories of task: "body tasks," such as collecting water and preparing food, seeking shelter in storms, and so on; and "spirit tasks," which are almost always periods of meditation (although there are some minor spirit tasks such as incense making and fire burning, as well). Body tasks are assigned to certain times of the day as appropriate, or as necessary in case of injury or other emergencies.

The remainder of the time in between is then allocated to spirit tasks. Thus, the days are filled with long periods of quiet reflection and meditation. Although meditation does not come naturally to me, I found that practice was the key to success; after trine sailing the sands, I became more finely tuned to the rhythm and the voice of the desert. Now, meditation comes more easily to me no matter where I am. In this way, I carry the Dousan with me, too.

THE XERICS

Like the Sifa, the Dousan do not live their daily lives in a single community, but instead are divided into many smaller groups. Among the Dousan, these close-knit groups are called xerics, each led by a sandmaster who has been trained and trusted by the Dousan maudra herself. Xerics are made up of between twelve and thirty Gelfling each, split into crews that pilot their sand skiffs. Larger xerics often employ the aid of a Crystal Skimmer—sometimes more than one—which improves their traveling ability, due to the Skimmer's sharp desert instincts and tireless endurance.

Out of necessity, the Dousan xerics are highly organized, with specific jobs assigned to small teams of Gelfling. Unlike the Sifan samaudren, which are formed out of the bonds of family or friendship, Dousan are assigned to xerics by the maudra and her council of sandmasters. These assignments are based on aptitude and skill. The day when a Gelfling is assigned to a xeric and leaves the Wellspring oasis is a very important day indeed.

Roles among the xerics vary depending on the size of the xeric itself, as well as the territory the xeric covers. All xerics are led by a sandmaster, and each sandmaster has two close companions—called second sandmasters—who have the knowledge and skill to take over for their leader in an emergency. They also serve on the xeric's council. All three of these leaders, the sandmaster and their two seconds, must agree on any important decisions before action is taken.

Two other important roles among the xerics are those of
pilot and navigator, who work together both in and out
of transit. The pilots are in charge of controlling the skiffs;
the navigators are seasoned sky readers and occasionally
far-dreamers with an eye for reading the constantly
changing crystal dunes. Among larger xerics that train
Crystal Skimmers for transportation, there is a second,
more specialized group of pilots who are able to direct
the Skimmers. The Skimmers are headstrong but loyal

beasts; it takes a great deal of bravery and fortitude to build such strong
bonds. Watching the pilots and navigators in action is exciting and almost
unbelievable. I marveled every day at their ability to exchange such large
amounts of information in such short periods of time using only hand signals.

Another role I found remarkable is that of guardian. When I first heard of the
Dousan guardian role, I imagined it to be something akin to the Stonewood
soldier or the like—a role focusing on defending the xeric and clan. While
these duties are part of the guardian's responsibilities—being skilled with a
knife and so on—the Dousan interpretation of the word *guardian*
could be more accurately defined as ritual guardian. A xeric's
guardian is responsible for delegating the daily spirit tasks,
and in many cases, acting as a mentor among the xeric. The
guardian is usually an elder and well versed in the many
meditations and practices observed and performed by the
Dousan; besides the two second sandmasters, a xeric's
guardian is the most well-respected member of a xeric,
and always serves on the sandmaster's elder council.

LIFE APART

My first encounter with any Dousan was in Cera-Na, where they sometimes come to trade with the Sifa before returning to their solitary lives to the southeast of the Claw Mountains. I was not sure, in the beginning, whether I would be able to travel with them as I had with the other clans; the ways of the Dousan are well guarded and not easily shared with outsiders. However, after some time with the sandmaster of a smaller xeric, I was able to explain myself: that I was a historian and song teller eager to learn the ways of all the seven clans. Open to this idea, the sandmaster suggested I accompany his xeric to the Wellspring and wait to speak with the maudra and her elders.

I lived in the Dousan's Wellspring oasis for some time before finally meeting the maudra, and I am glad that I did. She was enthusiastic about my quest, and looked among her sandmasters for an appropriate host to guide me and teach me the songs of their wisdom and long history. I was lucky enough to be assigned to a xeric with its own song teller—an infrequent position among the quiet, introspective Dousan. From this companion, and the rest of the crew of the xeric, I was able to see much of the Crystal Desert and its overwhelming beauty.

I had often heard that the Dousan were unfriendly toward outsiders—as are most Gelfling—but those rumors were, as rumors often are, largely ignorant. The truth I learned is much kinder: The Dousan's values and traditions do not prioritize connections with other Gelfling. Instead, they focus on their personal connection with Thra. Every daily action, every prayer, and every pillar of their community centers on this utmost directive. Their philosophy revolves around our mortal existence and the immortality of Thra and the Crystal.

Taken in this perspective, their aloof behaviors make much more sense. Their secretive-seeming ways are not secretive at all; their every action is personal and intimate, a relationship between each individual and Thra, which is no one else's business to know or to understand. Although this cultural difference was challenging for me at first—I grew up being taught to value my connection with my kin over all else—I came to appreciate it wholly. The Gelfling connection with Thra is one that could certainly be valued higher, especially among those Gelfling communities easily entrapped in daily social entanglements and political distractions.

LANGUAGE OF SILENCE

One thing that struck me about the Dousan that I had not encountered among other Gelfling was their silence. Where other Gelfling villages are always alive with some sound or another, be it speaking or laughing or singing, my time with the Dousan was consumed by an ever-present silence. When I finally asked Maudra Io about this, her reply was fascinating:

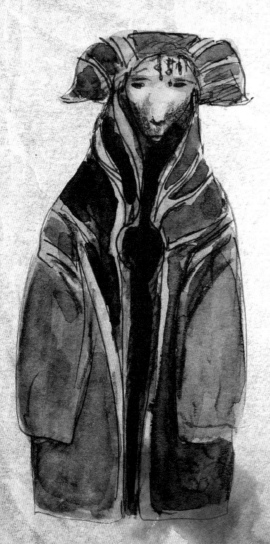

"Breath issues forth water from within the body," she told me. "Saving breath saves moisture, a valuable essence among the sands. In the beginning, this is why we learned as a clan to be quiet. But once we held our tongues, we found our ears were free. Open and undistracted, we began to hear the song of the sands, the song of the winds, the song of the Crystal Desert. When we became still, we were able to see how the world moves around us. When we devote our lives to silence, we become witnesses to the deafening melody of Thra."

For these reasons, the Dousan have a complete language of hand signals and are able to communicate just as fluently through these quick, articulate gestures as they are through words. They will often use this language—called *vojeye*—instead of spoken words, even in environments like the Wellspring where water is bountiful. I also loved watching Dousan signal at the same time as speaking; as I learned this beautiful, visual language, I began to understand the nuances of it, and realized how much more was being communicated when both hands and tongues worked together.

DAY OF THE DYING SUN

It seems most appropriate to remark upon the Dousan's observance of the Day of the Dying Sun, as their intimate relationship with the cycle of life and death is particularly apt in regards to the holiday of our dimmest and most fragile sun. On the single day that the Dying Sun is visible, the Dousan remove their head coverings and gather in threes. They clasp hands and perform what they call an "empty dreamfast"—a dreamfast filled with no memories or voices; a shared meditation of stillness and silence. They perform this empty dreamfasting for the entire time during which the Dying Sun is visible, ending only after it has once again dipped below the horizon.

The Dousan consider the Three Brothers to be three incarnations of the same entity—the Triple Sun—each representing a phase of life and death. The Dying Sun represents the decline of life and the journey toward death. In observing the Day of the Dying Sun in empty dreamfast, the Dousan share the journey with the Triple Sun's dying incarnation, if only for a day, and in that way are better prepared for the journey when they begin it themselves.

Trial of Daeydoim

There is a legend of a star that fell to Thra and was given a name by Aughra. Though the star believed itself to be of Thra for many trine, eventually it came to learn that it was from another world, one of the heavens above. And so, it came to question all it had learned, and wandered the desert for the rest of eternity. As it wandered, it left its footprints, and from those footprints sprang Daeydoim, a four-legged, shelled creature found only at dusk among the dunes of the desert.

The Dousan relate strongly to this myth. They refer to it often, and have taken the armored, sand-walking Daeydoim as their sigil creature. One of the most powerful observances of the myth is the Trial of Daeydoim, a gauntlet performed by any Dousan twice: first as younglings in preparation for leaving the Wellspring, and second as elders when they retire from traveling among the xerics.

The trial is simple in theory, though dangerous in execution: naked except for a simple sheet of red cloth, a Gelfling leaves the Wellspring in the dead of night. They are not to return for three days. On the third day, if they return—and not all do—they are anointed with the milk of the Wellspring Tree. If they are a youngling preparing to join the xerics, they are then allowed to stand before the maudra and the sandmaster council for their assignment. If they are an elder preparing to retire, they are granted their Last Home, a hut within the Wellspring, and a seat at the council circle.

I asked many of the Dousan what occurs within the three days of the trial, and what must be done by the Gelfling who is attempting to endure it. But this was sacred information not to be shared with an outsider, and so to this song teller, it remains a mystery.

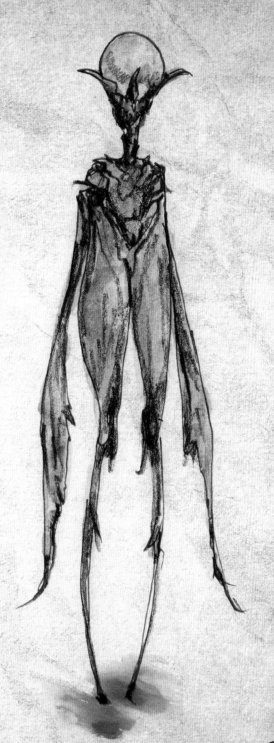

INCENSE

Though few Gelfling are fortunate enough to visit the Wellspring directly, Dousan incense is famous throughout the Skarith Land and among all the seven clans. It is burned in the Vapran Citadel in the chamber of the All-Maudra; I smelled it in the fires of Domrak in the Caves of Grot. It is said that even the Skeksis use it within their castle during ceremonies.

Dousan incense makers are strictly elders who have retired from their xerics, as incense making is a magic process that does not agree with the windy, fast-paced life aboard sand skiffs and Crystal Skimmers. Among the Dousan, incense is made in small, palm-size chips that are placed in torch wells and burned under enchantment until their blue-plumed smoke fills the air with its savory, heady scent.

The most traditional Dousan incense is made from dried bark peeled from the aging parts of the Wellspring Tree. Although it is mixed with other spices and scented substances—depending on the maker—the Wellspring bark is what gives Dousan incense its unique, irreproducible scent. The bark is dried and ground into a fine powder, and the mixture of dusts is compacted into

bricks using the sticky sap of the Wellspring Tree—an additive that lends an enchanting aroma that is not found in other incenses.

Then the bricks are left to dry in the arid conditions beyond the Wellspring's bounds. Large swaths of the sands just beyond the Wellspring Tree's shade have been cleared for just this purpose. Thanks to the sap and the experienced hands of the incense maker, the very fine dust dries rapidly, becoming extremely hard and packed. The bricks are then collected and carved into chips that can be easily brought to trade in Cera-Na and Ha'rar.

While spending time away from the desert, in the Wellspring, I tried my hand at apprenticing to a well-known incense maker. But I found I was not very skilled at such things. Despite following every instruction, my incense blocks were always too crumbly to be packed into bricks, though of course their scent was sublime. Perhaps when I retire, I will try again.

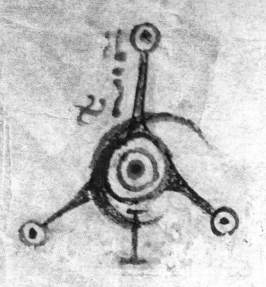

TATTOOS

The Dousan dress and adorn themselves sparingly and for function rather than appearance. However, in stark contrast to their minimal dress, most Dousan are tattooed, an appearance extremely uncommon among the other Gelfling clans.

While I was told by the Dousan tattooers that the tattoos block the glare and heat of the emboldened suns, the main purpose of the tattoos is in carrying meaning. Their shapes represent stories, and are performed by the elder sages at the Wellspring when the Dousan return from a particularly stirring adventure.

The tattooing process is long and painful, involving pots of inks, Crystal Skimmer scales, and a tiny mallet. Skimmer scales, shed by the creatures during molting seasons, have a prickly, spiny texture, and are about the size of a Gelfling palm. They are cut into strips and triangles and other shapes.

The scale shard is placed on the skin, spine side down, and struck with a mallet so the thousand spines prick the skin. Then, while the spines are still embedded in the skin, the bowl of scale is filled with drops of ink. The ink flows through the spines into the skin, and the scale is removed, leaving the ink embedded in the skin. However, the spines are not so closely knit that the ink coverage is very dense; the process must be repeated several times for each portion of the design to produce a rich, solid color shape.

Most of the inks used in tattooing are made from pollens and plant substances found within the Crystal Desert; the most common colors are deep blue, green, and gold, as these are all colors that can be made from the three varieties of crystal palm, which grow in abundance within the desert. Other colors can be harder to come by, such as silver and white. In these cases, the Dousan who desire these colors must procure the pigment materials themselves. This seeking out of tattoo dye substances is one of the few examples of materialism that I witnessed during my time with the Dousan.

FUNERALS

As sad as it may be, we Gelfling must all return to Thra someday. Believing themselves to be responsible for contemplating the mysteries of life and death—a responsibility given to them by Thra itself, according to the elders—the Dousan have created a life tradition around the inevitable. Meals begin by acknowledging the plants and animals that gave their lives so we might consume them. Meditation begins by becoming mindful and aware of our life force, and its mortal flicker.

Knowing all this, when one of the sandmasters of a fellow xeric met his untimely demise in a sandstorm, I expected the Dousan funerary rites to be somber. I was mistaken.

For the first time, my Dousan friends brought out their instruments. Pipes and drums and whistles that I had never seen them play before. We buried the fallen sandmaster in the soil beneath the Wellspring Tree, as all Gelfling must be returned to Thra. Then his xeric gathered his belongings and piled them in a pyre. The maudra lit it, and as the flames consumed what meager belongings he had possessed, the Dousan played a cascading song that ebbed and flowed and danced among the smoke and fire. The members of the sandmaster's xeric sang of their favorite memories spent with their friend. As they sang, the musicians played the song, bringing it to life within my mind as if by dreamfast. By the time morning came, the winds had scattered the ashes of the pyre, and nothing was left except the memories of the song.

FOOD

When I first ventured into the Crystal Desert with my Dousan hosts, I believed that I would starve. I knew this was not truly the case, since clearly the Dousan survive—in fact, thrive— in the barren-seeming land. But I had to set my doubts and preconceptions aside, and fully trust the xeric that took me under their wing as we set off into the desert, away from the woodlands and hills I am more familiar with.

Although the desert days are hot, the nights are almost unbearably cold. And under that cold cloak of evening, what little moisture exists in the atmosphere becomes heavy and falls to the ground, coating the sparkling sands in dew until the suns rise and it evaporates once again. Thus, every evening, the Dousan set out dozens of shallow water traps, which are then collected in barrels before daybreak, and in this way we always had fresh water to drink. Even so, our sips had to be rationed, but life in an environment where water vanishes in the day is all about self-control and restraint.

Where there is water, there is life. While the water traps fill, the Dousan slow their skiffs along pocketed dunes where reedy plants grow straight out of the crystal dust. During the day I mistook many of them for rock formations, but at night they explode with life. Enormous blossoms open along their entire bodies, and with the lovely scent come insects and birds and other creatures. Although the Dousan do not eat the flesh of any creature that moves during the day, they have no dietary restrictions on flowers. Raw spine-flower blossoms drizzled with nectar made from the flower's pollen are a delicacy among the southern xerics.

SONGS OF THE DOUSAN

I did not hear as many songs of the Dousan as I did among other clans. Although they certainly remember the art of song, it is not always functional in the desert, while living a life sworn to silence and meditation. However, there were some, and the few I was trusted enough to hear, I recorded (with the teller's permission, of course). One thing that is not conveyed among any of these written records is that Dousan song tellers perform with their hands as well as verbally. During performance of the songs, the language of silence used by the Dousan becomes a fluid, lovely dance—sometimes interpretive enough to convey entire stanzas and verses without a single word spoken aloud.

I did not become fluent in the Dousan's language of silence until late in my time with them. And so, it is with regret that I wonder how many of their songs I missed merely because I was listening and not looking. Perhaps one day I will have the opportunity to rejoin my Dousan friends, and with newer, older eyes see what I missed in my youth.

The Wellspring

Though the Dousan clan is separated into xerics that rarely convene all at once, the sandmasters do routinely return to an oasis located in the far north of the Crystal Desert—the Wellspring. It benefits from the shade of the cliffs as well as a spring of brilliantly clear water, and of course, from the tree that grows from the middle of the lake, casting its protective shade even on the brightest of days.

Here in the Wellspring, the Dousan restock their supplies of food and water, as well as tend to any ailing Gelfling who may need attention. Elderly Dousan leave their xerics when they can no longer remain agile enough to sail in stormy weather; it is here in the Wellspring that these sages retire, providing support for the xerics when they pass through, and maintaining the Wellspring itself.

There are numerous songs about the Wellspring sung by Gelfling of other clans who have had the opportunity to visit this wondrous place. It is fascinating to compare the songs of the Spriton and the Vapra to the songs of the Dousan themselves. I've provided a few examples of this below.

Verdant Paradise (Spriton Origin)

Verdant paradise showed itself to me
After wandering through the crystal sea
To my knees I fell in tears

Water quenched my thirsty tongue
Cool breeze told me I had come
At last to the safe haven

Where the Wellspring overflows
Where the Wellspring Tree grows
In this shade I rest forever

The Lovely Lake (Vapran Origin)

Oh, what lovely blue
Resting in the barren sands!
Like a sapphire true
In a traveler's shaking hands!

Oh, this lovely lake
Now I never need discover
In the crystal sands forsake
The desire for any other

These two short odes underscore the undeniable beauty of the Wellspring. But they also show their bias; a fear of the desert, as if the Wellspring is the only lovely place within the Crystal Desert. Compare these songs with one from the Dousan, which I first heard when we were several days' travel from the Wellspring. The Claw Mountains were barely a red line on the horizon, and our xeric had taken reprieve in the shade of a tall standing rock. My Dousan song teller sang this to us without an instrument except his voice and the tapping of his fingers on his knee.

Beloved Sea

Take me now into these gentle hills
Granules of crystal and bone
Sink me now into these soft blades
Take me home

Breathe me now into this cooling air
As the suns dip low
Awaken me now into the dark night
Where crystal flowers grow

Lose me now into my beloved sea
Enlivened with your might
Embrace me now, my beloved gem
Into endless light

As I listened to this heartfelt song, for the first time I felt in my breast the impossibly profound connection that the Dousan feel with the desert. In the Crystal Desert, the shifting sands of transformation are sudden and drastic. Life springs forth in the sands suddenly and is vanquished just as quickly. Accepting that our time here is short and death inevitable allows the Dousan to value the moment in which they are living, rather than becoming distracted and preoccupied with what could be or has been. Instead, my song teller companion sang of each grain of sand in the desert as a tiny crystal sprung from the Heart of Thra.

The Wellspring Cloister

Near the Wellspring, hidden among the red crags of the Claw Mountains, is a cavern temple carved by the Dousan over hundreds of trine. Here the Dousan pray to the Crystal of Truth, and record their wisdom and songs upon the walls. In many ways the cloister resembled the Grottan caves, a poignant reminder that our seven clans may not be as different as we have come to believe.

Though the Dousan have asserted to me that the Crystal can be addressed from any location (especially, though, from amid the crystal sands of the desert), the Wellspring Cloister contains an effigy of the Crystal: a large carved stone resembling the Crystal of Truth, the Heart of Thra, made of faceted, translucent stone. Having never seen the Crystal myself, of course, I cannot say if the sculpture is to scale; it stands some four times the height of a Gelfling, and is positioned in the center of a cavern under a hole that has been cut in the ceiling. When the light shines in, it seems to ignite the stone and the entire cloister.

As Dousan ritual requires, there are always at least three Dousan praying here at any given time. Losing moisture is of no concern here, where underground streams trickle in from the Claw Mountains and feed the Wellspring; and so, herein, I heard many chants and prayers to the Crystal that were spoken aloud as other Gelfling songs. Below is one such prayer.

Crystal Prayer

Shining in the light of the Triple Sun
Wherein the colored rays become one
Burst with sound unspoken
Resound with body unbroken

Your children chase your light
Walking in your shadow

The Wellspring Tree

Growing out of the freshwater lake in the center of the Wellspring oasis is a large tree, unmistakable from any direction as one approaches the Wellspring. I am told by the Dousan that the tree's broad leaves, sprouting from the very top of its crown, repel the lightning of the storms that frequent the rest of the Crystal Desert. These leaves, thick as the deck of a Dousan skiff, bleed a thick white milk when cut. This milk hardens into a stretchy, tough substance that is equally lightning repellent, used on the Dousan skiffs and clothing for protection.

The Wellspring Tree's origins are just as mysterious as those of the other patron trees. It is included in the many songs that say it was Mother Aughra who planted all seven. There are at least two Jarra-Jen tales that have alternative explanations. Yet another song claims it was two of the Three Brothers who are responsible, after falling to Thra. This song, one of the few fables told by the Dousan, is shared below.

The Two Brothers

Three Brothers chasing clouds across the sky
When two crashed and fell from the heights
Into the crystal sea

One a great guardian, big and strong
Two a navigator, rose and wan
Stranded in the crystal sea
They climbed the red mount's highest peak
They strained their arms but could not reach
From the crystal sea

The third Brother looked down and saw their plight
And sent word to their sisters of the night
The Three Sisters joined their hands and sang
And to their song the Crystal rang

Then up from the crystal sea
Sprang forth a crystal tree

The guardian and navigator, brothers two
Climbed the tree as it upward grew
Out of the crystal sea

And when they reached the sky once more
They looked down on the crystal shore
They saw the crystal tree sprung tall
Grown within the Wellspring walls

Tall and proud within the crystal sea
The guardian and the navigator's Wellspring Tree

In this song the Brothers are characterized as a guardian (the Great Sun) and a navigator (the Rose Sun), two of the most important roles among the Dousan xerics. Even more fascinating still is the visual depiction of these Brothers, which can be found in several places within the Wellspring Cloister.

There is one image in particular, showing two large figures standing beside what appears to be the Wellspring Tree in its sprouting stages. The two figures are decorated with halos, indicating their solar regency, but instead of taking a Gelfling form—as the suns often do when illustrated—the two Brothers appear to be almost Skeksis in shape, with long necks and tails and four arms each.

When I asked about this incongruity (remember, the Dousan do not regard the Skeksis as deities but as mortal creatures like Gelfling and Crystal Skimmers), the Dousan elders denied that the figures had any resemblance to the Skeksis Lords and claimed that any similarities were a result of my own projection and interpretation.

A Final Word

On my final days with the Dousan, I was escorted to the border of the Crystal Desert by the maudra herself. We rode her famous Crystal Skimmer, a brilliant gold specimen named Urami, whose lineage is said to go back to the Skimmer of the first Dousan who ventured into the desert.

I left my Dousan wards in silence, as is their way, and turned my back on the desert. I thought of the Trial of Daeydoim, and of the Gelfling course of life and death. Like that wandering star seeking a final resting place, I still searched for a path and a place I could not yet imagine. Yet if the Dousan are to be believed, it is the adventure that fills the place between birth and death that gives us purpose.

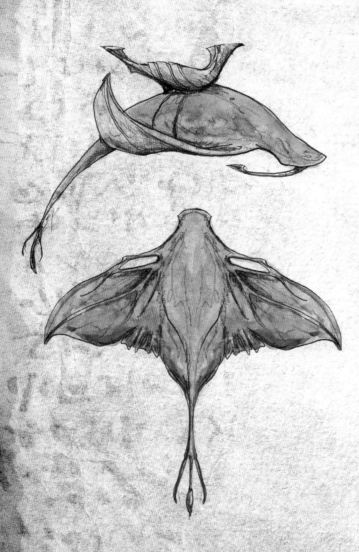

THE DRENCHEN CLAN

Great Smerth

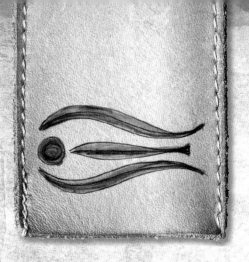

Far to the south, the plains give way to wetlands. These marshes, infused with the heat of the air, become more and more dense. By the time that solid land is all but a memory, the jungle and overgrowth are so compact, it can be difficult to see where one apeknot tree ends and the next begins.

Freshwater lakes make up the majority of the floor here in the Swamp of Sog, broken by raised tree roots and peaty mounds, punctuated by quicksand and gas vents.

Here among the giant apeknots is the largest tree in the swamp: the Great Smerth, with a trunk as wide around as a small village and hundreds of times as high. And indeed, this is where the Drenchen Gelfling make their home, with burrows carved with respect and care into the Great Smerth's living body. In fact, the Drenchen are the only Gelfling I visited who actually live within the patron tree of their clan. About seven out of ten Drenchen families make their home within the tree, with a minority living in hanging huts within the maze of its outer branches.

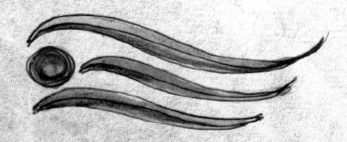

Although many Gelfling live separately from their sister clans, it could be argued that the Drenchen clan is the largest of these remote communities. In numbers, they rival the Spriton or even the Stonewood, but their distant and difficult-to-reach location limits their interaction.

Daily Life

The Drenchen are extremely organized, despite their number, performing every task within the clan in small groups that report to leaders within larger groups. A good example of this is how the hunting parties work. Among the maudra's council, there is an elder whose role is to manage the many hunting tasks necessary to feed the clan. She, in turn, has a small council of six Gelfling, each whom lead several hunting parties, each with their own captain. In this way, each of the smaller groups can always be assured they are working toward a greater purpose, ultimately that of the maudra and her council.

One thing I learned while living in Sog is how different the seasons are, and how this affects the daily life of the Gelfling who make their home there. Farther north, the seasons change from spring to summer to autumn to winter and so on. However, the snows of the northern regions never touch Sog; the temperatures rarely change from their warm and humid conditions; and it rains every day, sometimes without stopping between. So, while the Spriton and the Stonewood are preparing and harvesting and sowing crops, thinking in terms of the cycle of the trine, the Drenchen follow a different rhythm. Their hunting cycles follow the cadence of the quarry being hunted, whether that is migratory or spawning or something else. Their lovely hanging gardens, built into the canopies, bloom in every season, but require constant care if they are to bear fruit at the appropriate time.

Whether hunting, building, playing, or working, the Drenchen spend most of their time above the swamp in the apeknot canopy, called the High Road (of course, the muddy, unforgiving swamp below is thus called the Low Road). This was astonishing to me at first, since Drenchen wings are not as flightworthy as those of the Vapra and Sifa. Leaping through the gnarled apeknot branches seemed terribly dangerous without the safety of flight; yet the Drenchen are taught from a young age how to scale the tall trees and to read the stability of the apeknot branches and the distance between them. While the girls can use their wings to glide—lengthening their leaps by short distances or buffeting them enough to leap all the way to the swamp floor— even the boys, who of course have no wings at all, are always jumping to and from the boughs of the High Road as if it were as safe as skipping along a cobblestone path.

HEALING

Some Drenchen have a talent that seems to be unique among the Gelfling clans: that of healing the physical body. This is not an ability all Drenchen have, though it's not particularly rare, either. During the time I lived with the Drenchen, there were some dozen younglings with the gift, who attended regular training sessions with their elder healers, learning to control and focus their abilities.

What these healers are capable of is beyond remarkable. While the strength and finesse varies from Gelfling to Gelfling, with great care and the right mentor, it is said that any Gelfling can learn to use their gift to heal some of the most disastrous of injuries. As a testament to this, I witnessed a youngling mend a fractured bone—and her wings had not even bloomed.

Though the effects of this ability are undeniable, it is impossible to say where it comes from, especially as I have never seen it exhibited beyond the Swamp of Sog. Some songs say that the gift was learned from the Great Smerth itself when the Drenchen first made their home in the heart of the swamp. If this is the case, perhaps that explains why it is somewhat common among the Drenchen, but rare among Gelfling.

HARD-TALK

Among the Drenchen, especially at the elder council table, *hard-talk* is a phrase often spoken—especially in the rare instances when Gelfling from beyond the swamp are present. Hard-talk, meaning to speak without metaphor or hesitation, is an ability valued highly in Sog—though in my experience, somewhat ironically, as the Drenchen speak in symbols and with politeness just as fluently as any other Gelfling. So although the Drenchen may puff their chests when boasting how blunt and straightforward they are compared to other Gelfling, in actual practice I found hard-talk to be more of a communication strategy during serious debates. Essentially, as a key that opens the door to saying what others are reluctant to say.

For example, during challenging hearings in the maudra's council chambers, when it seems all have reached an impasse, an elder will forcefully stomp his foot and demand hard-talk. In this way, all present are excused from whatever potential insult they might bring by speaking their mind. This emphasis on honesty—and a promise of withheld judgment and a listening ear—has a fascinating impact on decision-making within the clan.

And while I thought perhaps hard-talk might cause strife and conflict, especially when elders or clan members are in disagreement with the maudra, I actually found the hard-talk tradition to strengthen trust in the elder council as part of the community rather than above it. I would be fascinated to see how such concepts might change the dynamic in other places where maintaining hierarchy is paramount, such as in the All-Maudra's court when the Skeksis Lords are present. It is my guess that Drenchen hard-talk would not go over quite so well.

MUSKI COMPANIONS

The swamp has created a hunting environment unlike any other. Though it seems overflowing with game and plants, the density of the foliage and the constant shifting of water make locating quarry difficult—and catching it even harder! Add to this the fact that quicksand and various predators are quick to snatch up game that is not collected immediately, and you have the makings of one of the most challenging hunts you will ever encounter.

To assist in these difficult hunts, the Drenchen have solicited the aid of the swamp Muski. These flying eels are indispensable as hunting companions, quick to retrieve quarry as well as bola. In exchange, the Muski partners take part in every aspect of Drenchen life, from travel to sleep to dining in Great Smerth's hall.

Unlike other companion animals I have witnessed during my travels, Muski seem to be very particular about choosing their partners, and once chosen, are bonded for life. Although some Gelfling have studied the Muski for generations and can predict the likelihood of a certain eel bonding with a certain Gelfling, it is impossible to make this guess with precision.

I was able to spend some time with an elder whose role was in matching Muski to Gelfling, and learned that one of the largest components of pairing Muski is in the precise timbre of the Gelfling's voice. Muski ears are very sensitive, able to pick up nuances in sounds that even Gelfling ears cannot perceive. Curiously, those who study the Muski have also found that certain spots and markings along the eel's body indicate what kind of voice that eel may be attracted to—thus, which Gelfling they may bond with.

Additionally, and perhaps related to the timbre of voice, Muski also seem to favor bonding along family lines. For example, the Muski bonded to the Drenchen maudra will spawn several times during her life, and it is likely that her offspring will be compatible with the maudra's children. Thus, many Muski bloodlines follow that of their Gelfling partners.

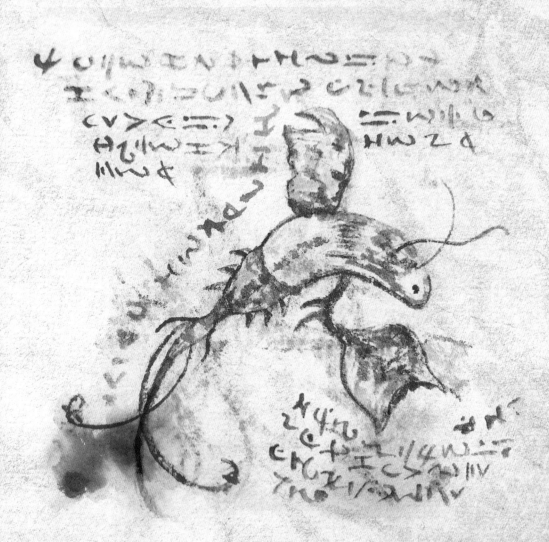

Spring Festival

The Drenchen observe most of the traditional Gelfling occasions, and even though seasons have a different effect on life in the swamp, as I've mentioned, those festivals marking the turning of the trine still occur with great consistency and enthusiasm. During my time with the Drenchen, I was able to take part in many a spring festival, which for me as a non-native to the swamp, was my favorite. Because flowers bloom at all times in Sog, they grow bigger and in greater numbers than in other places in the Skarith Land. Thus, when stringing the traditional flower garlands, it requires every youngling in the clan, and heavy ropes that can bear the weight of a thousand blooms in every color.

The spring festival is also the time during which the maudra's successor—as in other clans, usually her eldest daughter— addresses the clan in place of her mother, a great ceremony indeed, as it eases her into what will eventually be her role: standing before her clan and greeting them each, one

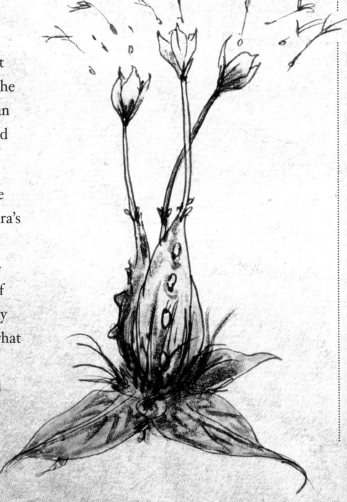

by one, and welcoming them into the new trine as they welcome her. She will then descend from the maudra's balcony and light the hearth that waits at the foot of the Great Smerth.

Once the fire is lit, the festivities begin, most of which are familiar to any Gelfling. Competitive games such as dart throwing and rope swinging are popular among the younglings, and of course for the adults, many of the vintners will introduce the trine's sogflower wines. As evening falls, the torches among the branches of the Great Smerth are lit, and the dancing and music will go on until dawn. The day following is often one of rest, granted to the entire clan in observance of spring and the vigorous and joyous activities of the day and night before.

Drenchen Drums

One of my favorite things about living with the Drenchen was waking to the sound of the drums. There is something particularly special about the way the beating resonates through the swamp in the earliest morning. I don't know if it is the way the sound reverberates against the apeknot canopy or the water or both, but there were many, many mornings I would simply lie with my eyes closed and listen.

Every morning, a single drummer signals the start of the day with a beat from among the arms of the Great Smerth, where large-skinned drums are fastened in clusters. The drums are so big and durable, the drummers use their spears to beat them—the thick and sturdy drumheads are not scarred even by the blue stone spearheads.

After the first beat of the drum, the rhythm steadily increases until it is similar to that of a Gelfling heartbeat. The other drummers will join the first after a

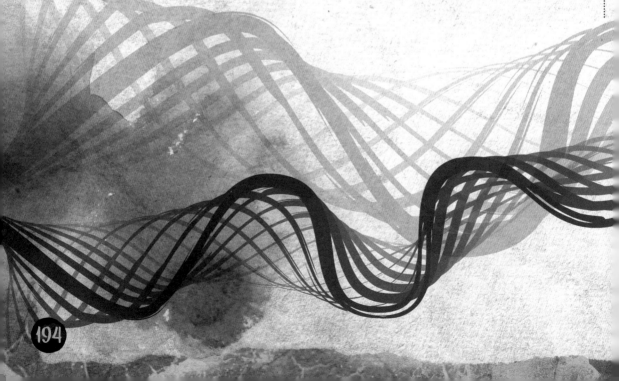

while, until the sound of the Drenchen heartbeat rings across the swamp. It is not just for the Gelfling of Great Smerth, but for the entire area that hears the drums. The birds begin their song, the swamp Nebrie coming to the surface to feed. The flowers that bloom during the day open their petals and fronds; those that thrive at night close up and rest.

The drumming will continue throughout the day. New drummers arrive in shifts, relieving their companions, so the drumming never ceases. The steady beat can be used by metalworkers and carpenters to moderate their strikes; the trembling can be felt below the water by the fish farmers and waterbed gardeners who work tirelessly to bring food to the Drenchen table. The beating can be heard by rangers and hunters who have gone out into the swamp, always calling them back home so they are never lost. This is the steady backdrop of life within Sog. The endless beating represents the community and its presence, as interwoven as the apeknot canopy.

WATERFASTING

While dreamfasting is a sacred bond between two Gelfling, there is likely
not one of us on Thra who has not wished to be able to dreamfast with other
creatures to understand their hearts and minds. The desire to do so, despite it
being an impossible feat, is what we call meditation: the attempt to connect to
the world around us through dreamfast, though our small Gelfling abilities are
unable to reciprocate the booming voice of Thra.

The Drenchen have a morning and evening ritual called waterfasting. Though
this is not observed by all within the community, many of the elders make
their way down into the lake at the foot of the Great Smerth to join in a group
meditation with the water. It is not uncommon to see small groups of elderly
Gelfling standing waist-deep in the lake, eyes closed, humming softly as they
move their flattened hands across the surface of the water as if in dreamfast.

I joined the elders many times, after I was invited, of course, and I found waterfasting to be a most meditative and relaxing experience. Though I was not able to enter the mind of the water, there was still something very reciprocal about the feeling of the gentle waves rolling under my hands. Especially when waterfasting with a small group, I could feel the projection of dreamfast emanating from my companions, as if we were creating a field of harmony that could truly be heard by the water. After spending many mornings waterfasting with the Drenchen elders, I must say I have no doubt the Crystal does, in fact, hear us. In its own way, even if that way is not the way of the Gelfling. Nay, it is the way of Thra.

THE MYSTIC BLUE

Although Drenchen art, whether weaving, painting, or otherwise, is often colorful (as many paints and pigments are available in the rich land of the swamp), I found the color blue was used much more frequently than other hues, especially in depictions of a mystic or spiritual nature. I counted roughly ninety dyes and pigments used in painting and weaving among the Drenchen artisans; of that ninety, nearly a third were shades of blue. Blue for the sky, for the water, for stone. Different blues for rain and for rivers and lakes. Made from fruits and vegetables, pollens and minerals, refined by colorists with great care and specificity.

This rainbow of blues can be seen in depictions of the Crystal, the celestial bodies, or Gelfling, for example. Drenchen Gelfling are always painted in blue, while Gelfling of other clans may appear in blue or other colors, depending on their narrative role within the work. The maudra's chambers are protected by hundreds of wood medallions, each with a sigil inscribed in blue ink. Blue eyes are considered a sign of mystical affluence. Indeed, when the sky clears and its blue face shows through the swamp canopy, the days are called mystic smiles.

Blue is also the color used when depicting fire, despite its naturally amber and red color. Fire, of course, is the most sacred of elements, representing spirit and the third eye. When illustrating fire of any kind—sacred or not—a particularly dark, rich, and shimmering blue is used, made from a mineral found within the swamp. The mineral is called *vliyaka*, named after Gelfling magic.

Hammers, a useful tool anywhere, but especially in the swamp, are made of blue stone, a variety of extremely dense rock common to Sog. While blue stone hammers are used mainly in construction, they are also crafted for ritual purposes, and often given as gifts. Drenchen song tellers say the tradition of the blue stone hammer dates back to Maudra Ipsim Vlisabi-Nara—also known as Ipsy the Blue Stone Healer. This title is passed down to the Drenchen maudra generation after generation.

FOOD

Though traditional Drenchen meals are predominantly composed of fish and fresh game, there is no shortage of fruits and vegetables in the swamp. Thanks to this abundance of variety, my meals were never boring when I was living with the Drenchen in Sog.

One thing I found unique and wonderful about the Drenchen was their style of eating. It is called *dotraba*, which means "big table," and perfectly describes this communal style of meal. In *dotraba*, dishes are prepared in bountiful quantities and served on large platters that are used by all who sit at the table. In this way, mealtime becomes a community event, and everyone is invited to share and to feed one another as well as themselves. Mealtime among the Drenchen was always joyous and energetic, and everyone was always well fed.

The *dotraba* style becomes more interesting when all the Drenchen—not just small groups, such as families—gather on special occasions in Great Smerth's dining hall. This chamber is large enough to fit nearly all the Drenchen of the clan, and during these *dodotraba*—very big tables—the dishes are brought out from the kitchens by the chefs one at a time. As each platter is finished by the group at the table, another arrives to replace it. And, as the Gelfling become sated by the meal, they retire to the kitchen to begin preparing the next round of platters, thereby relieving those who were so recently cooking and serving. When I asked about this tradition, the Drenchen maudra Elaia told me that *dodotraba* is not just a method of eating, but a symbolic ritual representing the unending cycle of life and death.

FISHERIES

Fish is used in many of the Drenchen's most popular meals, especially during spring, when the Blindfish spawn. To maintain fish numbers, the Drenchen keep underwater fisheries below the Great Smerth. These fisheries provide safe habitats for the fish, as well as allowing the Drenchen to count their numbers and, in turn, moderate their harvest.

The fisheries are constructed of lake stone, mined from the swamp bed, and aligned in concentric circles. If one were to stand among these small walls, they might come up to one's knee. The Blindfish are mud-dwelling, and rarely swim higher than the walls, so they remain within the fisheries at peace, while simultaneously being easy to harvest for the Gelfling fishers who swim down from above. The curvature of the fishery tracks also prevents the fish from panicking, as the walls block water disturbances and sound vibrations.

The fisheries are broken up by covered stone huts, which provide dark caves for the fish to bury themselves in. These shadowy sanctuaries are also where the fish deposit their eggs and where the young hatch.

SOGFLOWER

Of particular delight is Drenchen sogflower wine, made from the pollen of a large flowering water plant that grows in huge numbers within Sog. When water levels are low, the flowers remain dormant. However, during rainy seasons, the flowers shoot up from the swamp beds on fast-growing stems, with the bulb of the flower developing just below the water's surface. Then, as the water levels drop, the flowers spring open, ready to be pollinated. They remain open for only a short time, the flower's stems unable to support the heavy blossoms when the water level is low. The stems then break or bend down from the weight, shedding their spores into the water for the next generation.

Thus, every time the water levels begin to drop, the Drenchen gathering parties travel into the swamp with large pouches and collect the sogflower stamens, heavy with pollen. This pollen is then reduced by the Drenchen apothecaries into a fine, very sweet syrup, which is mixed with various juices rendered from swamp fruits, and fermented. The result is a delicious wine with the consistency of mead, the delight of any Drenchen gathering.

Sogflower, like many of the flora native to Sog, also has medicinal and healing properties. When the pollen is made into a salve or paste, it prevents infection in cuts; sogflower wine is also used generously in the curing of illnesses, as it calms the body and mind while simultaneously promoting hydration.

SONGS OF THE DRENCHEN

Drenchen, Masters of Water

Perhaps the most remarkable thing about the Drenchen, which sets them apart from all other Gelfling, is their ability to breathe underwater. They are the only Gelfling known to have gills, and while their wings are too small and dense for flying, they make unparalleled fins for maneuvering underwater. Watching them swim in the lake at the foot of the Great Smerth filled me with envy; I can only imagine how much of our world will go unexplored by those who cannot pass below the surfaces of the lakes and rivers and oceans.

Like their healing abilities, the origin of the Drenchen's gills is a mystery. And, as we know, mysteries are the source of many a song. The following is one of the Drenchen's favorite folktales, often sung during rain festivals, when the water levels are high enough that the sogflowers bloom.

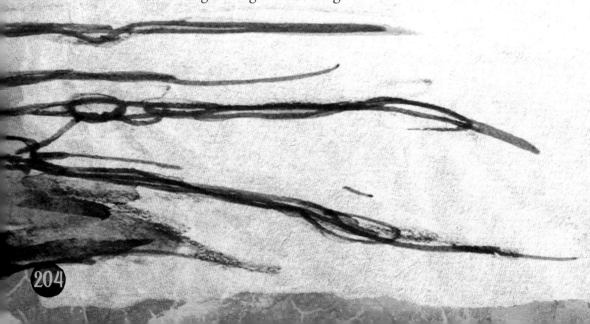

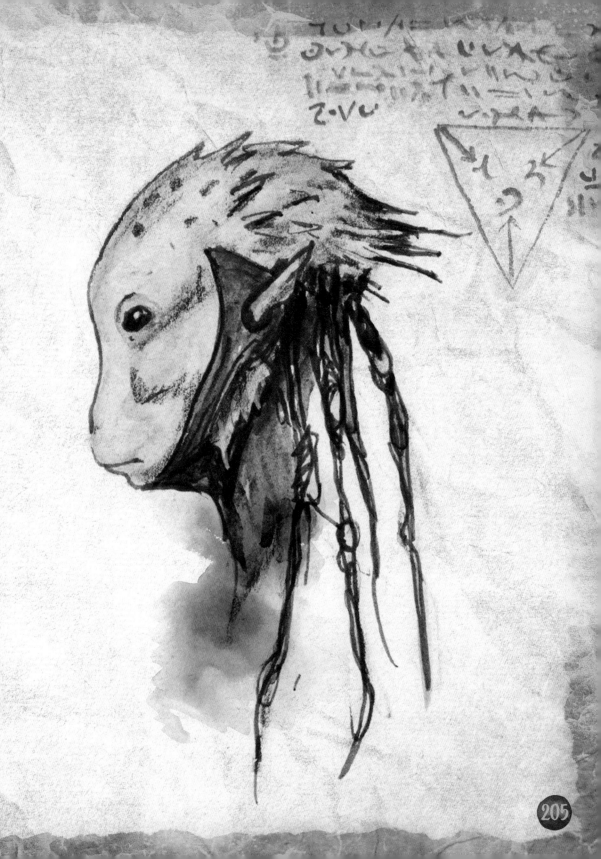

205

While the tree in the song is often assumed to be the Great Smerth, other songs say that it was, in fact, Mother Aughra who planted the seed that would later grow to be the Drenchen's patron tree.

Ipsy and the Great Seed

Yea, do you remember the trine far past
When the first Gelfling came to Old Sog
Yea, they traveled so far for a place to rest
A home to be made out of apeknot and bog

Oh, Ipsy was the name of the maudra back then
And young though she was, she was brave
She saw future in Sog, saw a place to call home
In this tangled and dangerous glade

The water was high as it always was then
And the Gelfling, they drowned one by one
As they tried to survive in the treacherous place
Slowly but surely they were overcome

The Gelfling told Ipsy she must take them away
Before the waters devoured the last of their clan
But Ipsy did not know where else they would go
Where else they could live in the Skarith Land

So Ipsy went off into the deepest Sog
To find the answer to their desperate need
She promised to return in three days' time
Three days later she returned with a seed

The Gelfling gathered round when Ipsy returned
Three fewer than when she had left
They watched as she buried the seed in the moss
Then fell to their knees and wept

"Oh, Ipsy, Thra's failed us," cried they to her
As the swamp licked their ankles in waves
"If this seed is the answer it's offered to you
This terrible place becomes our watery grave"

But Ipsy had heard the great whisper of Thra
She believed, for she had to—and sang . . .

Light blossomed forth from the seed in the moss
The Gelfling sprang back in surprise and in fear
In moments a sapling had burst from the ground
And it whispered a promise in young Ipsy's ear

Then the great tree grew out at a quickening pace
And into the waters the Gelfling were thrown
But as they gave up their last gasping bubbles of air
They found that they had not drowned

"Care for me as you'd care for your mother"
said the tree as they breathed with new lungs
"And I will care for you as my children
My dearest Drenchen ones"

And the Drenchen Gelfling promised at once
Breathing the water into which they'd been freed
They danced under the surface in the shade of the tree
That had sprung from young Ipsy's great seed

Giant Apeknots

Apeknots are trees that grow only in the Swamp of Sog. Their porous roots and trunks capture air, allowing them to survive even in areas which are completely submerged in water. As they grow, their branches reach out parallel to the water below, connecting with the fronds of other apeknots until the canopy is one interconnected web of leafy branches. The same is true of the apeknot root system. In this way, all apeknots are part of one living, breathing entity that embodies the entire swamp.

Of course, when anything is such an important part of daily life, it eventually becomes immortalized in song. There are dozens of Drenchen odes to the apeknots that form both the pathways and the latticed roofs of their beloved swamp; here is one sung by childlings as they practice counting.

Three, Six, Nine

One, two, three
Hop, skip, leap
Four, five, six
Leaf, twig, stick
Seven, eight, nine
Climbing up the vine!

One, two, three
Up the apeknot tree
Four, five, six
Mind the nesting chicks
Seven, eight, nine
Climb a second time!

One, two, three
Along the apeknot tree
Four, five, six
Hear the Muski cricks
Seven, eight, nine
Climb a third time!

. . . and so on. Childlings are challenged to invent their own stanzas as the
song goes on.

Spear Breaking

Spears are the instrument of choice among the Drenchen, closely followed by the Drenchen bola. However, spears are used in ceremony just as frequently as in hunting, as the spear represents spirituality (the blue stone head) and mortality (the wooden shaft). Spears are crafted by their bearers, usually under the supervision of an elder, and carried for as long as the spear itself can endure.

When a spear shaft finally cracks or bends—inevitable, of course, in the moist and rigorous conditions of daily Sog life—a tradition called spear breaking follows. During this short yet requisite ritual, the spear bearer breaks the shaft fully (if it isn't already) and removes the spearhead. The broken shaft is discarded into the lake to rejoin Thra, and the spearhead is transplanted onto a new shaft. The tradition is often observed by close friends of the spear bearer, and is ritualized thus:

Spear-Breaking Incantation

Bend to my hand and break
Thra, my body take
Renew me now my mind
Leaving the old behind

Spear shafts are usually inscribed by elders with sigils of bodily protection against injury, illness, and other physical harm. The spearheads are left uninscribed. Instead, as they withstand action, either during hunt or ritual, any marks left (often temporary, as blue stone is nearly indestructible) are immortalized using blue dye. The spearheads belonging to elders are often almost completely blue after their owners' many trine serving, hunting, and teaching within the community. When a Drenchen passes, their spear shaft is ceremonially broken by the maudra and buried with them. The spearhead— the existing proof of their spiritual influence within the community—is hung among the hundreds of others that dangle in the Great Smerth's canopy. When the wind blows, you can hear their gentle, low-pitched song. I myself wrote a short song in ode to this.

Spirit Stones

Remember souls long past
Broken though their bodies be
Listen and you'll hear their fast
Spirit stones among the canopy

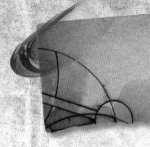

Smerth-Staba, the Sogwood Tree

Some songs say that the Great Smerth, the Glenfoot Tree, is the originator of all the apeknots within the swamp; other songs say that after the swamp rose from the mud and marsh, three magnificent apeknots grew together in a braid at the heart of Sog and became the Great Smerth. These two origin tales have one thing in common: heralding the Great Smerth to be the largest apeknot in the swamp. It is no wonder the Drenchen have chosen it to be their home.

Within the air-filled vasculature of the Great Smerth's body, the Drenchen have gently, over many trine, made their homes. When I walked within the corridors of the magnificent tree, I could hear the footsteps of many tip-tapping against the wood. It sounded like the heartbeat of the tree itself. As the Drenchen tend to the tree that is their home, one can easily hear the sigh of love and relief that the tree breathes in return. The glowing warmth emanating from its heartwood is proof that it thinks of the Drenchen as its children.

The following is a hymn sung by the Drenchen maudra thrice a trine to honor the Great Smerth. This song is performed before the entire clan. I had the honor of witnessing it during the autumn equinox. The entire clearing was quiet and still, not a single bird interrupting the silence as the maudra stepped out onto the balcony overlooking the clearing. She turned to face the tree, her solitary voice sending chills up my back as she paid homage to the tree that protects her clan.

Drenchen Maudra's Song to Smerth

O come, blue flames, from our very breath
O come, blue stone, from the very earth
O come, blue wind, to this Drenchen place
O come, kneel us down before the Great Smerth

Behold all we have without taking any
Behold all we are with your gentle face
And come blue skies and the bluest springs
O come, kneel us down in this sacred place

Arugaru, deatea
Kidakida, deratea

A Final Word

I left the Drenchen on a spring night to the sound of the beating drums and music in my honor. It was joyous, although bittersweet; my shoulders were sore from the friendly jostling, my belly full from *dotraba* earlier that evening. The glowing plants among the apeknots lit my way through the canopy, the Drenchen drums accompanying me long after I had left the glade at Great Smerth. And even when their booming faded, I could feel my heart was soothed and overflowing with love and generosity, and would remain so for many trine to come.

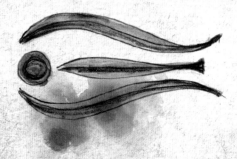

TO END IS TO BEGIN

And so here, after many unum of sleepless nights writing, I finally find a place to lay my quill to rest. My hand is aching, my second finger callused. My palm stained with ink, and my mind alive with the memories awakened by this writing. As if dreamfasting with my own past, if only so I might pour out those dreams into a cup from which someone else may drink.

I began a simple Stonewood song teller who wished to see the world. To find her own path, and to understand her place in the world. For her own ends, perhaps; perhaps it was a selfish quest in the beginning. But now I know what may have begun in self-service has ended in the opposite. I thought in the beginning there were Stonewood legends and Spriton myths, Sifan ballads and Dousan chants and Grottan hymns. Drenchen drums and Vapran choirs.

But now I know better. I went searching for my path and my place, and found songs along my journey. And those are what I bequeath to you now.

So, take these words. Take these songs. Take these memories, and hold them in your hand. See in them the faces of the many Gelfling who live beyond you, hear their voices and how they join the chorus that is the Song of Thra. Raise this cup and raise your voice; drink deeply and exhale with your own melody.

Find yourself drawn into the song, where you join the others whose songs you know now as well as you know your own. Know that whether you are Stonewood or Spriton, Drenchen, Sifa, or Vapra, Grottan or Dousan, you are always Gelfling. And perhaps more importantly, now, know that you are a song teller. As I am and was; as I now bless you to be. Take these songs and know this; go forth and sing them with a voice loud and clear.

For no matter which path you travel, that song is the Song of Thra; and it is the way home.